MARVEL

BLACK PANTHER

UPRISING

BLACK PANTHER
UPRISING

RONALD L. SMITH

MARVEL

LOS ANGELES • NEW YORK

First Edition, September 2022
10 9 8 7 6 5 4 3 2 1
FAC-004510-22203
Printed in the United States of America

This book is set in Adobe Caslon Pro, Century Gothic/Monotype;
The Hand/S&C Type
Designed by Catalina Castro

Library of Congress Cataloging-in-Publication Data on file
ISBN 978-1-368-07300-4

Reinforced binding

Visit www.DisneyBooks.com
and Marvel.com

For Rosie Lee Smith
Beloved mother & Number One Fan

CHAPTER ONE

T'Challa couldn't stop thinking about barbecue.

Not just any old barbecue, but a stuffed sandwich dripping with tangy sauce and a glass of sweet tea to wash it all down. A hot bowl of Southern mac and cheese would be nice, too. Maybe even a corn dog.

Instead, he stared at the plate of food in front of him: leafy green vegetables, freshly peeled plantains, a bowl of kola nuts, and a few slices of flatbread. He wasn't too impressed. Last year, he had spent the summer in Alabama with his friends Zeke and Sheila, and had eaten so much Southern food he was now craving it.

He sighed.

His trainer, Themba, had been putting him through his paces for a week straight. T'Challa felt like he'd never worked out so hard before in his life: five miles every morning followed by core work and a cool-down period using Kemetic yoga, which was all about centering yourself through breathing exercises. This was a reward of sorts, after such a hard session, and T'Challa always came away from his workouts refreshed and calm.

He tried some of the plantains, chewing thoughtfully and savoring the taste, when he was interrupted by a knock at his door. T'Challa paused.

Who could that be?

No one came near the Prince of Wakanda's residence without close inspection. Whoever was on the other side had already been vetted by his guards, that was certain. T'Challa opened the door and was met with a smiling face.

"M'Baku. What are you doing here?"

"Huh?" M'Baku asked, practically bowling T'Challa over on the way in. "Do I need a special invitation to see the prince?"

T'Challa closed the door and shook his head.

He and M'Baku were the best of friends, and had been since they were little kids. But their friendship wasn't always sunshine and roses. It was put to the test a while back, when the two boys visited America for the first time. M'Baku had fallen under the sway of a charismatic student named Gemini Jones and his gang, the Skulls. T'Challa soon found out that they were more than just a street gang. They were a secret society, operating out of their school and trying to summon dark magic. What followed was a nightmarish adventure that ended in a deadly confrontation with a supernatural entity. It took T'Challa a while to forgive M'Baku for his part in all of it, but they soon became friends again, and had left their previous dustup in the past. Still, M'Baku had a way of testing T'Challa's nerves. Like now, for example.

M'Baku walked around at his own pace, picking up items and putting them back down. He was a big teenager, and his size seemed to take up all of the air in the room.

"Looking for something?" T'Challa asked.

M'Baku inspected the underside of a small panther figurine. "No, not really. Never know what kind of royal stuff you have hidden away. Any new tech to try out?"

T'Challa sat back down while M'Baku thumbed through several books. "Nope. I left my invisibility suit in the science lab."

M'Baku's mouth fell open. "In . . . *visibility*?"

"Gotcha!" T'Challa exclaimed, and burst out laughing.

M'Baku frowned. "Knew that sounded too good to be true."

"Serves you right," T'Challa teased him, "for being so nosy."

M'Baku finally flopped onto one of the chairs and released a heavy sigh, although he still eyed the room as if T'Challa were hiding treasures. It was an unassuming place for a prince, but if one were to look more closely, a marvelous blend of nature and technology would be revealed. The floor was woven bamboo reeds covered by soft fabrics. Vivid watercolors depicted scenes of the Wakandan landscape. A flat-panel monitor—where T'Challa watched American movies when he got the chance—took up most of one wall. Earthy brown wood carved into intricate shapes made up the furniture. The beauty and craftsmanship of Wakanda was reflected in every object—from simple knives and forks to the straw baskets that held fresh fruit.

"So, what are you up to today?" M'Baku asked.

"I have to spend a little time at the Academy," T'Challa replied. "Father says I'm a good role model for the students, so he wants me to make an appearance at least three times a week."

M'Baku scoffed. "I'm sure they'd rather be racing around on hover bikes than listening to you drone on about being a prince."

T'Challa shot his friend a sardonic grin. He was used to M'Baku's barbs, and wasn't offended in the slightest. "Well, it's important for them to learn about Wakanda and its history, too, right?"

M'Baku shrugged.

The students at the Academy for Young Leaders, more commonly known as the AYL, were the best and brightest Wakanda had to offer. In a few years, they would be applying for roles in the government as assistants, hoping to one day land a prime job in the Wakandan cabinet. T'Challa was glad to be a mentor to them.

"Well," M'Baku said, "the Festival of the Ancestors is coming up in a few days. That should give you a break. All of Wakanda's gonna be partying!"

T'Challa bit his lip. He had almost forgotten about the Wakandan holiday, which made him feel a little guilty. It was a day of celebration and remembrance, a tribute to Wakanda's noble ancestors, ending in a ceremonial display honoring Bashenga, the first Black Panther.

All of Wakanda was awaiting the day.

But not all for the same reasons.

CHAPTER TWO

T'Challa and his family lived in the Royal Palace in Birnin Zana, the capital of Wakanda. The private compound was a sprawling complex with rooms for the royal family and their close advisors. This was the seat of power and where T'Challa's father, T'Chaka, the ruling Black Panther and King of Wakanda, led tribal council meetings and listened to the concerns of the other Wakandan tribes. His security force, the Dora Milaje—a group of fierce women warriors trained in weaponry and martial arts—kept close watch on the comings and goings twenty-four hours a day.

T'Challa always felt a bit smothered in the palace, like he couldn't really be himself. The halls were quiet and solemn, and the highly polished black onyx floors gave a sense of power to those who walked them. Security was everywhere. T'Challa felt like he couldn't even go to the kitchens for a midnight snack without an entourage at his heels.

But we're at home, he had complained to his stepmother, Queen Ramonda, several times. *I would think we'd at least be safe here, without security following us around.*

Sometimes there are threats even from within, T'Challa, she told him.

T'Challa took his stepmother's words to heart. She was a wise woman and the only mother he had ever known. His birthmother, N'Yami, had died bringing T'Challa into the world. He thought of her often and wondered what his life would have been like if she had survived childbirth. Then again, he told himself, Ramonda was the best mother a child could ever hope for: strong of heart and mind, and a fierce protector of her children and her nation, including T'Challa's little sister, Shuri, born to Queen Ramonda and his father, T'Chaka.

T'Challa thought back on her comment about his father having enemies. Who in Wakanda would want to harm his father? Life in the capital was peaceful, and people had all the comforts they could ever ask for.

After turning thirteen, T'Challa felt he needed his own space, and decided to do something about it. But it wasn't as easy as he might have thought. It took a little convincing for his father to finally allow him to move into an area of the palace farther away from the rest of the family. It was only a short distance, but to T'Challa, it felt like a thousand miles and gave him the little bit of freedom he craved.

Of course, his younger sister, Shuri, thought this was unfair, and campaigned for her own place as well, but her father and Queen Ramonda didn't budge. *Maybe in a few years,* they said. Shuri sulked for days, and shot eye daggers at T'Challa every time she saw him.

T'Challa said good-bye to M'Baku and headed to the AYL. His ever-present security force, the Royal Guard, kept watch as he walked. Usually, the Dora Milaje accompanied members of the royal family everywhere, but T'Challa had argued that he couldn't be himself with them hovering over him at all hours. Sometimes, he thought, their fierce gazes and no-nonsense demeanor kept everyday Wakandans at a distance, and, more than anything, he wanted to be treated like "one of the people," even though he knew that was far from the truth. As a compromise, his protection was divided between the Dora Milaje and the somewhat more staid—but just as dangerous—Royal Guard, devoted loyalists who had served the family for generations.

It was another sweltering day in Wakanda, and the streets were overflowing with vendors, musicians, and pedestrians. Even though the capital city was a testament to futuristic design, touchstones of traditional African culture were everywhere—from the colorful clothing and headdresses to the open-air food markets. But mixed within the landscape were technological marvels that would make American engineers and architects envious: high-speed maglev trains, self-driving vehicles, shops with holographic storefronts, and so much more. T'Challa often wondered what it would be like for his friends Zeke and Sheila to see his home. Then again, he realized that was an opportunity they would probably never have.

T'Challa entered the building that housed the AYL and peered skyward. Slanted rays of sunlight poured in through a massive glass ceiling ribbed by Vibranium beams, bathing the whole place in a golden glow. He paused a moment to take in the grand view. It was spectacular.

After a moment, he found the class and paused in front of the closed door. One of his security guards knocked once and then entered. T'Challa hated this part. His "Advance Team"—as his father called the Royal Guard—had to first clear the way before T'Challa made an appearance in front of an unvetted group. *But they're just kids my age,* T'Challa thought. *What could I have to fear from them?*

T'Challa heard murmuring through the closed door. The guard came back out, gave him a nod, and then held the door for him to enter. The class immediately stood to attention amidst a scuffling of shoes on the floor. Professor Silumko, a tall man with a gleaming bald head, gave a brief nod. "Thank you for coming, Prince T'Challa. We are honored to have you as our guest."

T'Challa swallowed hard and waved to the students in

a friendly gesture. A sea of expressionless faces stared back at him. He felt self-conscious, as if the whole world was studying him. He shoved his hands in his pockets, like that would help.

"We were just discussing Wakanda's place in the modern world," Professor Silumko said to T'Challa as the class once again took their seats, "and how we must always continue to evolve."

T'Challa tensed. Was he supposed to say something? Give a lecture at the drop of a hat? He shifted on his feet.

"But what about the ways of our ancestors?" a boy called out. "They didn't have Vibranium back then, but they were still able to build a society and thrive."

A few other students nodded in agreement. Professor Silumko clicked the pen he held in his closed fist. "Thank you for your comment, Tafari. In this class, as you well know, it is customary to raise one's hand when asking a question."

Tafari half rolled his eyes and slunk down in his chair.

T'Challa studied him. He had an inquisitive, owlish look about him, made all the more distinct by his wire-framed glasses. He was about T'Challa's age, but smaller and leaner, and wore very simple clothing—a dashiki with bold red-and-green patterns and a necklace of beaded stones that formed an oval around his neck.

"My prince," Professor Silumko said, turning to T'Challa, "would you care to comment on Tafari's observation? What can you tell us about our country's founding before the discovery of Vibranium?"

T'Challa steepled his fingers together in front of his chest in what he thought was an academic pose. He tensed. *I have to get over this fear of public speaking. I have to lead one day. I can't do that without talking!*

"Well," he began, "our ancestors were a very strong people. They accomplished a great deal as a society before Vibranium became our most valuable resource."

Tafari raised his hand, grudgingly, it seemed to T'Challa.

"Yes, Tafari?" Professor Silumko asked wearily.

"Right," Tafari said. "And we were a better nation *before* Vibranium. Now we have everything we could ever imagine. But we have lost the one thing that is most important."

"And what would that be?" Professor Silumko asked.

Tafari rose up in his seat. "Our connection to the past."

The room fell silent. T'Challa swallowed. He was intrigued by Tafari's comment. Wakanda did have everything one could ever hope for in a society: wealth, peace, prosperity. But what did it all mean? What did it add up to?

Professor Silumko let out a labored breath. "Our history is important, Tafari, but so is progress. Without it, you wouldn't be here, right now, in this very school, with the best teachers in the nation."

"But what about our neighbors?" a young woman asked, raising her hand at the same time she spoke. "Shouldn't we be more generous with our resources? We have poor nations all around us, but we sit on our bounty of precious Vibranium while the world around us suffers."

Nods of agreement all around.

T'Challa gulped. He wasn't prepared for this type of debate today. He just wanted to make a quick appearance and go about the rest of his day. It seemed like the students had other things on their minds.

Professor Silumko began to walk down the aisle, and paused in front of the student who asked the question, a girl with tight cornrows and a gem in her left nostril. "There is much that Wakanda does that goes unnoticed by our people, Aya. We have programs in place that give aid to our more peaceful neighbors: food, agriculture, educational resources."

"But *not* our technology," Aya countered. "Our Vibranium."

"True," Professor Silumko said. "That is what sets us apart. We must always maintain our advantage."

T'Challa recalled conversations he'd had with his father much like this one. The king told him that being the only country with a wealth of Vibranium came with great responsibility. If they shared their precious metal too widely, a less stable nation could use it for nefarious means, and that was something the King of Wakanda would not allow.

"The Festival of the Ancestors is just a few days away," Professor Silumko said, coming back to stand in front of the class. "There is no better representation of Wakandan strength and our rich history."

Tafari shook his head in what T'Challa thought was frustration. "The Festival of the Ancestors is an empty display meant to celebrate our culture, but our true history is lost to the ages."

T'Challa felt heavy tension in the room, like a thundercloud ready to burst. Professor Silumko audibly exhaled.

"Not true," another girl said. "We all know the story of Bashenga. He was the first Black Panther and King of Wakanda."

"He was a warrior shaman," another boy put in, a note of pride in his voice. "A mystic. The leader of the Panther Cult."

"True," Tafari said, and a smirk suddenly formed on his face. "Blessed by the almighty Bast herself."

T'Challa eyed Tafari curiously. He detected sarcasm in his voice and wondered what it meant.

Professor Silumko looked defeated. His brow creased. He turned to T'Challa. "Thank you, my prince, for visiting us today. It is a great honor."

T'Challa was taken aback by the quick end to the debate. He gave a weak smile. The room was quiet. "Thank you, Professor. It is my pleasure."

As he left the room, he felt Tafari's eyes on his back.

CHAPTER THREE

Preparations for the Festival of the Ancestors were underway in the capital. The festivities were to take place near the Great Mound, where, every day, workers mined for rich veins of Vibranium. Machines and drones did most of the heavy work, but some Wakandan citizens still did hands-on tasks, like sifting through the rubble of blasted rock to get at the smaller deposits.

T'Challa took in the sights as he strolled through the streets, his guards a few feet behind him. He really didn't like that he had to be followed everywhere. It made him feel too privileged, and he sometimes wondered what ordinary Wakandans really thought of him. Did they think he was spoiled and entitled? A snob? Tafari certainly seemed to think so, even though they hadn't spoken directly. He didn't appear to be a fan of the royal family, at any rate.

T'Challa tried to understand what Tafari was getting at. Did he really believe Wakanda would be better off without Vibranium? What would T'Challa's life be like without the otherworldly resource that gave the nation so much power?

His thoughts were interrupted by the sheer magnificence around him. It wasn't often that he was out and about, especially given his royal status, and he took a few moments to really soak in the city's beauty. The smell of food rose on the air, courtesy of the many vendors plying their trade. On any given day, one could try every delicacy the nation had to offer—from roasted meats and decadent sweets to vegetables that the larger world thought long gone. Wakanda's agricultural crop specialists had brought back the foods of their ancestors through heirloom seeds and cuttings, offering up a bounty of culinary delights to a new generation.

T'Challa continued to walk, taking in the sights and enjoying the fresh air. Long ago, Wakanda had given up fossil fuels and pollutants. Vibranium was the resource that powered the nation. He looked up as a drone flew silently overhead. It reminded him of when he was a little kid, and his father had taken him for a ride on the Royal Talon Fighter—the king's personal aircraft. T'Challa was thrilled and ecstatic at all the tech on board. There were weapons, of course, and payloads of deadly arsenal, but there were also the matte-black surfaces, the sharp smell of heat and power, the dials and daggers that jumped to attention when the Vibranium-powered ship rumbled for takeoff. The view from thirty thousand feet was an experience he would never forget.

A group of students on hover bikes zipped by, sending one of T'Challa's guards into a tirade about "today's kids." T'Challa had to chuckle. A few short years ago, he was one of those "kids." Now, at thirteen, he had more responsibilities, even though he still longed to run barefoot through a moonlit forest, or catch a fish and roast it in the open air for supper. Whether he liked it or not, he was becoming the man his father raised him to be: the future King of Wakanda.

T'Challa slowed as his guards came to flank him.

People were approaching.

It was another entourage, he saw, so the person they concealed had to be someone from his own family or one of his father's close advisors. A moment later, he saw who it was.

"Hey, big brother!" his sister, Shuri, called.

T'Challa smiled and greeted her as they drew closer.

Shuri was young but had already proven herself an asset to Wakanda. She was a prodigy when it came to science and math, and had even contributed several ideas to the scientists in the engineering labs.

"What are you doing?" she asked.

"Just 'taking the air,' as Father says."

Shuri smiled and made a stern face that was supposed to

be an imitation of their father. One of her guards shot her a disapproving look. Shuri stuck out her tongue at him.

"Ready for the big fest?" Shuri asked.

"I suppose so," T'Challa answered.

"I was thinking about going as Bast," Shuri said. "I had some of the engineers in the design group create a panther costume. It even has glowing blue eyes!"

T'Challa winced. He wasn't sure what to think of his sister dressing up as the Panther Tribe's goddess. Sure, his father's suit and the one T'Challa owned were modeled on Bast's appearance, but Shuri had quite the imagination, and might want to add her own creative touches. Like glowing blue eyes.

Blue eyes.

A quick vision of a dark tunnel and brilliant blue eyes cutting through the murk flashed through T'Challa's mind. The memory was still fresh.

Run, Young Panther. Run.

He thought back to when he had visited his friends Zeke and Sheila in Alabama. The first few days were great, and he had learned all about the American South: its food, people, and customs. He even had a few reflective moments where he questioned Wakanda's wealth and power compared to some of the poorer parts of America. A few days in, however, the pleasant trip turned into a true nightmare.

T'Challa and his friends had discovered that one of his father's old adversaries, the Reverend Doctor Michael Ibn al-Hajj Achebe, also known as Bob, was wreaking havoc in a small Alabama town and planning a mass abduction through hypnosis and fear. In the events that unfolded, T'Challa had found himself in some sort of underworld, where he faced a creature called Chthon, only to be saved by what he thought was Bast herself.

Run, Young Panther. Run.

The experience still shook him to his core.

"Hey," Shuri said, yanking her older brother's arm. "Are you listening? Wakanda to T'Challa?"

T'Challa came back to the moment.

"C'mon," Shuri pressed him, grabbing his hand. "I want to show you something."

"What is it, Shuri? I don't really have time to—"

But he was dragged away before he had a chance to finish.

Shuri led T'Challa through the busy, noisy streets, their guards a short distance behind them. As they walked, several Wakandans laid a hand on their hearts in greeting, or raised and crossed their arms on their chests. T'Challa nodded and returned the smiles and well-wishes. He turned back to Shuri. "Where are you taking me, little sister?"

"Almost there," Shuri insisted. She turned around to face him. "And don't call me little!"

T'Challa smiled. He had no choice but to follow. When Shuri had a mission, she focused on it like a laser. T'Challa's security guards fussily checked their watches, as if T'Challa was on some sort of strict schedule, even though he wasn't.

Finally, after several minutes, Shuri led him to a place he knew very well. It was called the Oasis, one of his favorite spots to spend time alone. He loved the wild reeds and the butterflies and hummingbirds that made it their home. In the summer, the breeze was fragrant with jasmine and lavender. Dragonflies hovered above the water, their multicolored wings reflecting sunlight like stained glass.

They came to a stop. T'Challa wiped his brow. "Now what?" he asked, looking around. "Why'd you bring me here?"

Shuri only grinned and turned away from her brother. She peered into the distance, which was full of botanicals, tall reeds, and blooming shrubs. "Okay," she called. "You can come out now."

T'Challa literally scratched his head in confusion.

Low-hanging tree branches parted, and two people stepped out.

T'Challa's breath caught in his throat. "Zeke? Sheila? What in the world are you guys doing here?"

CHAPTER FOUR

T'Challa stood still. Shocked.

They couldn't really be here, could they? How?

Before he had a chance to say anything, one of his guards tapped a bead on his Kimoyo Bracelet. "This is Leopard One to Base. Seeking information on two—"

"I already cleared it with my father," Shuri said, cutting him off. "You know . . . your king?"

The guard seemed to shrink where he stood. He tapped the bead again. "Disregard."

Sheila and Zeke stepped forward and they all exchanged quick hugs. T'Challa's head was spinning. "How are you here? Who authorized this? You can't just . . . walk into Wakanda!"

"Actually, we flew," Zeke said. "It was Shuri's idea."

T'Challa turned to his sister, his face still a mask of confusion.

"Yes, I must admit," Shuri said, as if confessing to a crime. "I've seen you, big brother, when you think you're alone."

T'Challa raised a questioning eyebrow. Zeke snickered.

"What?" T'Challa asked. "What are you talking about?"

Shuri shifted on her feet. "I mean, I see the pressure you're under . . . how Father's always giving you lessons about how to rule. I knew you needed a break from your princely duties."

She gave an exaggerated bow, which only made T'Challa feel more embarrassed in front of his friends.

He swallowed. His sister sure was perceptive. Lately, his father had been talking to him more and more about the responsibilities that would one day rest on his shoulders. The king thought he was helping his son prepare for the day when that would become a reality. Actually, it only made T'Challa feel unsure of himself.

He laid a hand on his sister's shoulder. "Thanks, Shuri. This really means a lot."

"Right," Shuri said. "You can pay me back later."

T'Challa rolled his eyes.

A sudden rumbling overhead made them all look up.

Zeke's eyes grew wide as a high-tech airborne craft passed through the clouds. "This place . . . this place is like . . . geek heaven!"

T'Challa chuckled and smiled while his guards stood tense and alert, as if somehow, Zeke and Sheila were spies ready to steal state secrets. It was a rare thing to see outsiders in their secretive African nation.

"That's one way of putting it," Sheila said.

T'Challa and Shuri led Zeke and Sheila back toward the palace. Every few moments his friends would stop and stare, awed by the landscape and everything it contained.

"It's what I thought it would be," Zeke said, "but also different. If that makes sense."

"I know what you mean," Sheila put in. "It's . . . amazing."

A loud cowbell clanged in the air, turning everyone's heads. T'Challa saw Zeke and Sheila staring and followed their gaze. A shepherd dressed in simple clothing had stopped traffic to allow his flock of sheep to cross the street. A floating image of a news screen hovered in the air from his wrist, courtesy of a Kimoyo Bracelet, an accessory that every Wakandan possessed.

"Now I've seen everything," Zeke said.

"Kind of a culture shock, huh?" Shuri declared.

"But it seems right," Sheila said. "Like, this is how it's supposed to be."

"There's a lot more to see," T'Challa promised them.

A short time later, they were all in T'Challa's room, where they took seats on cushions and chairs. Zeke and Sheila looked dead tired, but their eyes were filled with awe. One of the beads on T'Challa's Kimoyo Bracelet pulsed red. He tapped it, and an image of his father's face appeared in a 3D hologram.

"T'Challa," King T'Chaka started. "I take it Shuri showed you the surprise?"

"Father!" T'Challa gasped. "This is unbelievable! How did you plan all this without me finding out?"

T'Chaka gave his son a rare smile. "Well, I *am* the king."

T'Challa wanted to pinch himself, but he knew it was really happening: His two best friends—friends who had been with him through thick and thin—were sitting in his room, thousands of miles from their homes.

"Shuri never let up on her plan to get them here," King T'Chaka said. "You know how . . . persuasive she can be."

A mischievous grin lit up Shuri's face. "Don't say I never did anything for you, big bro."

"Now, there are limitations," King T'Chaka warned them, his face suddenly stern. "Your friends are guests, but they have to remain with you and Shuri at all times. Sorry, T'Challa. That's just the way it has to be. I had to convince my advisors to authorize this visit, so I want you all on your best behavior. Stay close to home, and no wandering around unsupervised. Understand?"

"Yes, Father," T'Challa replied.

Zeke's face was frozen while looking at the King of Wakanda. "Thank you . . . oh mighty king," he managed to blurt out.

Sheila closed her eyes in embarrassment. Shuri giggled.

Sheila turned back to the hologram. "Enkosi," she said, dipping her head.

King T'Chaka smiled. "Wamkelekile, Sheila. I'm sure you'll be fluent in Xhosa in no time."

The hologram winked out.

Sheila turned to Zeke. "It means thank you," she said, anticipating Zeke's question.

"Nice way to make an impression," Shuri said. "Father appreciates hard work and education."

"I just wanted to learn a few basic words before we came," Sheila replied.

A soft knock on the door drew their attention.

"Come in," T'Challa called.

The door opened and M'Baku walked in. He looked at Zeke, and then Sheila.

He paused.

"What are you two nerds doing here?"

Zeke and Sheila were given small apartments in the palace, next to T'Challa's. Since they were friends of the prince, anything they wanted was only a call away. A security guard stood outside their door at all hours, which was something T'Challa told them they'd just have to get used to.

"This is . . ." Sheila started, as T'Challa showed them their two rooms, "the coolest apartment I've ever seen."

"It's got everything you'll need," T'Challa said, "and a few other things, too."

Zeke and Sheila took in the room, their eyes still wide from meeting King T'Chaka. There was a transparent TV screen, a floor that shifted from cool to hot depending on the temperature of the soles of your feet, and wall panels that you could swipe like a tablet to find the perfect backdrop. "It's like laptop wallpaper," Zeke exclaimed, "for your wall!"

T'Challa showed them a small black disc, about four inches in diameter, which contained controls for everything from opening and closing blinds to playing the sound system. The beds were ergonomic pods, built for the perfect night's sleep. By the time T'Challa was finished showing his friends around, they were flabbergasted.

"Imagine what a place like this would cost in the States," Zeke said.

Sheila snorted. "I don't think that comparison's even possible. For one thing, our latest tech is still light-years behind Wakanda's."

Zeke eyed a small black button over his bed. "What's this do?" he asked, reaching out with inquisitive fingers.

"Don't touch that!" T'Challa snapped.

Zeke quickly drew his hand away as if he were about to touch a hot stove.

T'Challa sighed a breath of relief.

"Jeez, Zeke!" Sheila whisper-shouted. "You can't go around touching things you don't understand!"

Zeke ducked his head like a turtle's going back into its shell.

"It's a security system," T'Challa explained. "If you had pressed that button, the outside of this building would have been immediately shielded by a Vibranium force field. The Dora Milaje would have been here in seconds."

"Dora what?" Zeke asked.

After T'Challa explained the king's security force, Sheila said, "We could use some women like that back in the States." She gave Zeke a side-eye. "When men are acting like fools."

"I'll see if I can get you an audience with them," T'Challa jested.

Zeke stifled a yawn with his hand. "Sorry. I'm pooped."

"Me too," Sheila said.

"You guys get some rest," T'Challa told them. "Tomorrow, I'm giving you a tour."

"Yeah," Zeke said, yawning. "Sounds cool. Can't wait."

A few minutes later, he fell asleep in his chair.

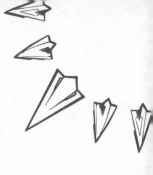

CHAPTER FIVE

On Zeke and Sheila's first full day in Wakanda, T'Challa took them out to explore the city. Unfortunately, Sheila's request to see the science labs was denied. "It's on my father's off-limits list," T'Challa told her.

Sheila was crestfallen. "I understand. Just thought I'd at least try."

They weren't allowed inside the throne room, either, much to Zeke's chagrin. "Wanted to see the Panther Throne," he said, pouting.

"It's not really a throne," T'Challa told him. "It's more like—well, I guess I can't tell you that, either!"

Zeke sighed.

"What about food?" Zeke said with renewed enthusiasm. "You need to turn me on to some Wakandan cuisine!"

T'Challa chuckled. Zeke was as skinny as a fence post, and he often wondered where all the food he ate went.

"It's not like Alabama," T'Challa told him. "The food is different here, but it's good once you get a feel for it. And, generally speaking, Wakandans don't eat as much as Americans."

"I'm up for anything," Zeke said. "My stomach's rumbling!"

"I know just the spot," T'Challa said.

A short time later, T'Challa led them through a densely packed street teeming with activity. Street musicians with drums and kalimbas played alongside kids engaged in a 3D holographic game. The pieces floated in midair as people traded banters and boasts. A floating screen beside them showed their strategic moves. Zeke and Sheila couldn't stop staring.

"What are they doing?" Sheila asked.

"It's called Kharbaga," T'Challa said. "Kind of like checkers. Older people like to use the traditional board and pieces, but people our age like to play in virtual three-D."

"Cool," Zeke whispered.

Sheila jumped aside as a girl with a pink Afro zipped by on what appeared to be a skateboard.

"What the . . . ?" she started.

"Oh, man," Zeke said, turning around and trying to get

28

a closer look. "It's floating. I mean, it's levitating! How in the world . . . ?"

"It's maglev technology," T'Challa explained. "The whole city has magnetic tech running underground."

"I need one of those," Zeke said wistfully as the rider disappeared down the street.

T'Challa continued to lead his friends through the city. Wakandans did double takes every time they passed, and whispered to one another conspiratorially. Not only was the prince out for a stroll, he had two friends with him as well, and, according to their clothing, they were *not* from Wakanda. Soon after, rumors began to swirl that they were members of a powerful American family, or, some said, young geniuses from abroad. Whatever the reason, Zeke and Sheila drew attention wherever they went.

T'Challa was still a little shocked that his friends were here in his own country. "Tell me again how you guys got here."

"Well, we were told to go to O'Hare Airport," Zeke said. "Once we got there, a man—one of your people, I suppose—showed up and drove us to this big airplane hangar in the middle of nowhere."

"And inside that hangar was a plane," Sheila added. "That's the one that brought us here."

"What about your parents?" T'Challa asked. "Where do they think you are?"

"That was the funny part," Zeke said.

"Somehow," Sheila began, "your father, or whoever was arranging our visit, made it look like some kind of all-expenses-paid student-exchange program."

"Like when you and M'Baku came to Chicago," Zeke added.

"We have no idea how they did it," Sheila put in, "but our parents were cool with it."

T'Challa shook his head in amazement. "How did you guys keep it a secret, with our video calls every week?"

Sheila grinned. "Zeke almost spilled the beans several times. I had to keep him in check."

"I'm not very good at secrets," Zeke confessed.

T'Challa gave him a side-eye.

Zeke suddenly wilted. "I mean, I've never said anything about Wakanda to anyone, though."

"But I'm sure he'd like to brag to *someone*," Sheila put in, "if he could."

"Would not," Zeke shot back.

"Would too," Sheila said.

"Guys," T'Challa scolded them. "We're here."

The redbrick façade before them was covered by a mural of a human figure with the head of a panther standing among tall green reeds. A single unmarked door was the only entrance. T'Challa looked back to his guards. "We won't be too long," he said, to which one of the guards nodded.

Zeke sniffed the air. "Something smells good!"

Sheila twitched her nose as well. "It does smell . . . enticing."

T'Challa didn't respond, but pulled open the door.

"Wow!" Zeke whispered.

The space was a long rectangle with recessed lighting on the ceiling, casting down shades of red and green. Three large stone-slab tables took up one wall. On one side, an open kitchen revealed chefs hard at work over open flames. The smell was incredible.

"Prince!" a voice called out.

A second later, a young woman rushed out from the kitchen and greeted T'Challa and his friends.

"Gloria, this is Zeke and Sheila," T'Challa said. "Two friends from— Well . . . they're just friends. They wanted to try some local cuisine, and since you're the best chef in the city, I thought I'd bring them here."

Gloria didn't look too much older than T'Challa. She wore her hair short and her smile was as bright as the rings that glittered on her fingers. Pink sneakers could be seen below her chef's apron, which showed an image of a cat with extremely long whiskers. She turned her gaze to Zeke and Sheila and studied them for a moment, as if trying to figure them out. "Well," she finally said, "you brought them to the right place. Any friend of our prince is a friend to us. Have a seat, and I'll have some drinks brought out."

After being led to a table, Zeke and Sheila took in the

place. "So," Zeke asked, "is this, like, some kind of private restaurant?"

"Not really private," T'Challa replied. "But it is . . . exclusive."

A man with long dreadlocks brought a tray of drinks to the table and set it down. He gave a quick hand-on-heart to T'Challa and disappeared back into the kitchens. T'Challa picked up one of the ice-cold glasses, filled to the rim with a thick, dark liquid.

"What kind of drink is it?" Zeke asked.

"Try it," T'Challa suggested.

Zeke and Sheila picked up their glasses. Sheila took a long swallow. "Ahhh," she said. "Refreshing."

Zeke followed suit and then let out a small burp. "Oops!" he said, and immediately covered his mouth. "Tastes familiar."

"Kola Kola," T'Challa said. "From kola nuts."

"Wow," Sheila put in. "I had no idea."

"America has a lot of foods and drinks that originated here, in Africa," T'Challa explained.

A rhythmic, trance-inducing tune with percussive beats piped through the speakers. Sheila bobbed her head to the music.

"This is like some kind of hipster club," Zeke said, drumming his fingers on the stone table.

"Not that you've ever been in one," Sheila pointed out.

"I've seen a lot of music videos, though!" Zeke shot back.

A minute later, the table was swarmed by several kitchen staff offering small plates and drinks. Gloria pointed everything out. It was a feast: Kalahari truffles, sweet yam soup, hot flatbread dusted with nutmeg, oven-roasted chickpeas, spicy jerk chicken. Dessert was something called Malva pudding, a sweet and spongy cake with notes of vanilla and apricot. It was all washed down with more Kola Kola and red bush tea made from rooibos leaves.

Zeke pushed away his empty plate and sat back and exhaled. Sheila did the same. She was a vegetarian, and was glad the meal wasn't a meat festival, like it might have been down South, where her grandmother lived.

Gloria appeared and surveyed their empty plates. She crossed her arms. "I'm sorry you didn't like my cooking."

"That," Sheila started, "was one of the best meals I've ever had."

"*The* best," Zeke said.

"Thank you, Gloria," T'Challa put in. "It was excellent."

"Anything for our prince," Gloria replied. She glanced at Zeke and Sheila. "I'll see you and your friends at the festival?"

T'Challa froze. He suddenly realized he hadn't told them about the festival yet. "Yes," he said. "I'm sure they'll be able to go."

"Festival?" Zeke said. "What festival? Will there be food there?"

Sheila put her head in her hands.

CHAPTER SIX

In the days that followed, T'Challa and M'Baku showed Zeke and Sheila all around the city—at least the places that the king had approved. His friends were awestruck.

"Wakanda," Zeke said breathlessly, looking out at the slopes of Mount Bashenga, a towering peak that rose into the clouds. "So that's where all the Vibranium is, right?"

"Yes," T'Challa whispered, out of earshot of his guards.

"Never thought I'd be a tour guide," M'Baku complained, but in a friendly tone.

Earlier, M'Baku had made an apology of sorts to Zeke and Sheila for his past behavior in America. He had been

34

rude and bullying to both of them the whole time he was in Chicago, calling them "nerds" whenever he got the chance.

"I was a fool," he said now. "Sorry about that."

"You weren't the only one to fall under the spell of Gemini Jones," Zeke said.

"I know," M'Baku replied. "You guys and T'Challa were right, though. I should have listened. It was childish of me."

"Everyone deserves a second chance," Sheila pointed out.

"Thanks, guys," M'Baku said.

T'Challa listened without adding a comment. He was glad that the three of them had gotten past the awkward relationship they'd had in Chicago.

"What's going on in Chi-Town, anyway?" M'Baku asked. "How's the pizza? I loved that deep-dish."

"Same old, same old," Zeke replied. "Cold and gray."

"The Windy City," M'Baku said. "I remember that wind. 'The Hawk,' they called it."

"Some say the name came from the long-winded politicians," Sheila explained, "and not the cold wind."

"Interesting," T'Challa put in.

"Not like here," Sheila said, as she turned her face up to the sun, enjoying a rare cool breeze that suddenly stirred around them. "I love that you have the best of nature and city life all in one place."

"Ah," T'Challa said. "That gives me an idea."

"What?" Zeke and Sheila asked at the same time.

"It's a secret," T'Challa said, "and you're just gonna have to trust me."

M'Baku shrugged. "I'm in."

"Us, too," Sheila added.

T'Challa looked his friends up and down. "Only one thing."

There was no reply, only eager faces.

T'Challa smiled. "I hope you brought some hiking shoes."

An hour later, after a quick stop to pick up water bottles and a few other supplies, Zeke and Sheila, along with M'Baku and T'Challa, found themselves in a deep valley with soaring white-stone cliffs above them.

"This is the Valley of the Kings," T'Challa told them. He had ditched his guards before they had set out, something he had only done a few times before. He'd be scolded for it, that was certain, but the last thing he wanted to do was to explore Wakanda with his friends while his security detail tagged along.

The sun was high, and Zeke and Sheila wiped sweat from their brows. "This is amazing!" Sheila exclaimed.

M'Baku, who knew the area well, was taking pictures using his Kimoyo Bracelet. "Some say this valley is where Bashenga, the first Black Panther, and his tribe initially settled."

Zeke searched the ground as if he could find some kind of treasure from Wakanda's past.

"It had a different name back then," T'Challa said. "That is, if I remember my history correctly." He pointed up to the cliffs on either side of the valley. The remnants of broken towers and columns could still be seen. "Up there, some say there was a mountaintop city called Bastet, where the Panther Tribe was first formed."

"*And* that they could actually turn into panthers," M'Baku added.

Zeke froze where he stood. He looked at T'Challa. "Please tell me this is true," he demanded.

"I'm sure it's just a story," T'Challa said, "passed down from generations ago. An origin myth, they call it."

"You never know," Zeke said. "Maybe you should try to turn into one when you take the throne!"

T'Challa shrugged. He didn't even like using a phrase like *take the throne*. It wasn't that simple. He would still have to prove himself in ceremonial combat when the time came, like his father and all the Black Panthers before him. *Will I be found worthy?* He shook the thought away.

"Just a little farther," T'Challa urged them. "I want to show you guys something."

Zeke and Sheila adjusted the packs on their backs and followed T'Challa and M'Baku.

The ground beneath their feet wasn't dry, but verdant

with moss and wildflowers. Even the air itself was refreshing this low in the valley. Zeke pointed at a herd of gazelle in the distance that seemed to sense their presence and then leapt away.

T'Challa bounded up a small hill of rocks.

"I need more fuel," Zeke demanded. "What's for dinner tonight?"

But before he could get an answer, cool air suddenly caressed their faces, accompanied by a whooshing sound like wind and rain blended together.

"What is it?" Sheila asked.

As they rounded the corner, the answer was revealed.

Sparkling torrents of water cascaded from a magnificent waterfall so high it seemed to disappear into the clouds.

"That," Sheila started, craning her neck up, "is . . . I don't even have the words."

"Let's get a little closer," M'Baku suggested.

There wasn't an actual path, so they had to walk around or climb over large granite boulders. It took a while to make their way up, and Zeke scraped his knees several times. "No one said this would be a workout," he complained.

"Almost there," T'Challa said, feeling a little sorry for his friends. The climb was an easy chore for him, as he was used to pushing himself, so he slowed a little, giving his friends a chance to catch up. Finally, they navigated their way up a mound of black rock and green grass to stand in a little rocky cove where the water fell in front of them like a curtain. A fine mist speckled their faces as they took deep breaths of the cool, refreshing air.

"Hello!" Zeke shouted, cupping his hands around his mouth and listening to his echo bounce back.

Sheila ran her fingers along the damp reddish moss that clung to the rocky wall. "The flora and fauna here are so different," she said, her face just an inch away from the wall. "It's like nothing I've ever seen before."

"Some people say the Valley of the Kings is a mystical place," T'Challa explained.

"Cool," Zeke said, looking around in wonder. The wet mist made his face slick, and he pushed his glasses up on his nose.

"Now," Sheila said, "if only I could get some samples. That would be—"

"Can't let you do that," M'Baku cut her off. "Right, T?"

"I'm afraid he's right, Sheila," T'Challa confessed. "Some of the flora and fauna in Wakanda still bear the effect of Vibranium radiation, from all those years ago when the meteor crashed. I doubt my father and his aides would let you guys out of Wakanda with any kind of . . . contraband."

Zeke scoffed. "Contraband? It's, like . . . moss, dude!"

"Who knows what power . . . mere moss holds?" M'Baku said in an exaggerated, spooky voice.

Zeke laughed.

"Well," T'Challa said, "you know how you can't bring certain things back into America after you've been abroad?"

"Yeah," Sheila replied.

"It's kind of like that. You could be transporting some mysterious strain or virus that could turn deadly. Like a pandemic or something. You never know."

"Attack of the Moss People," Zeke quipped.

They all sat and rested for a while, enjoying the respite from the Wakandan sun. T'Challa leaned back against the rocky cliff wall. He searched in his bag and passed around some sweet dates and dried papaya. He hadn't been to the Valley of the Kings in years. He and M'Baku often came here when they were younger, sneaking away and getting into trouble upon their return. He missed those days, when he was just a kid. Now everyone treated him like the future king. *What will I do when it is my time to rule?* he wondered.

"We should be getting back," M'Baku said, "before your guards abandon their search and tell your parents you're missing."

T'Challa gulped, suddenly concerned. "Yeah. I guess you're right."

He stood up, and his friends followed his lead. After filling up their bottles with fresh water, they headed back down, carefully maneuvering around the boulders. The Wakandan sun was still high, and T'Challa looked up to see a large bird with a massive wingspan flying low through the valley. "Look!" he shouted.

"What is it?" Sheila asked, shading her eyes from the sun.

"It's called a kori bustard," T'Challa said. "I've never seen one before."

"It's Africa's heaviest flying bird," M'Baku put in.

The bird faded into the distance with slow, heavy thrusts of its wings.

"Amazing," Sheila whispered.

They approached the bottom of the valley again, angling their bodies sideways to prevent themselves from tumbling downhill.

"Look who's here," a voice called out as they reached level ground.

T'Challa turned around. He tensed. A group of people were approaching. They were kids. But they looked . . . *odd* to T'Challa. For starters, they were all wearing simple white robes, like holy people on a pilgrimage. One of them looked familiar to T'Challa. After a moment, he placed where he had seen him. It was Tafari, the boy from the AYL. He was with the girl who had spoken up in the professor's class— Aya, T'Challa thought she was called. He hadn't even heard their approach.

"Who are they?" Zeke asked quietly.

T'Challa didn't reply because he was so taken aback by their clothing. He offered Tafari a friendly, awkward smile.

Tafari didn't return the favor.

M'Baku eyed the group warily. "You know them?"

"Not exactly," T'Challa said under his breath. "I sat in on a class they were in at the AYL."

Tafari took a few steps forward so he was facing T'Challa. "We saw you at that restaurant earlier," he said. "Afraid there's no fancy food out here, though." He turned to his friends. "That's how the royal family is, you know. They get whatever they want, *whenever* they want." He paused and looked at Zeke and Sheila for a long moment, studying them. "Hope you enjoyed your meal. Not everybody in Wakanda gets to eat like that."

Tafari lowered his voice and let out a flurry of words in Xhosa. His friends snickered. T'Challa couldn't hide his shock, and shook his head in disgust.

Sheila and Zeke turned to look at each other, both of them dumbfounded.

"How did they know where we ate?" Zeke whispered, but M'Baku stepped forward, interrupting Zeke.

"You do know who you're talking to, right? This is the prince, the son of the king. *Your* king."

Tafari and his friends smirked. "We know who he is," Tafari said.

"What are you doing out here, anyway?" M'Baku pressed him.

Tafari held up his hands in mock innocence. "What? Us?

We're just enjoying Wakanda's natural beauty. Wakanda is for all of us, right?"

Zeke and Sheila stood quietly, taking in the scene.

"I think we better get going," T'Challa said. "C'mon, guys."

"Good idea," Aya called out. "You should head back to the palace. Wouldn't want your royal robes getting dirty."

M'Baku flexed his neck. "All right," he said, stepping forward. "Now you've disrespected my friend, and, more importantly, the prince."

"Disrespect?" Tafari scoffed, moving closer. "What has your prince done to *earn* respect? Besides being born with a Vibranium spoon in his mouth?"

Sheila audibly gasped.

T'Challa felt as if he had been slapped in the face. He didn't know what to say or do. He stood there, struck frozen by nothing more than a comment.

M'Baku slung his backpack off.

Tafari seemed to take the measure of him, sizing him up. He stepped forward two inches, his white robe flapping. "You wanna go, big man? Let's do it."

Zeke and Sheila backed up a few steps.

T'Challa reached out and grabbed M'Baku's arm. "No," he said. "Leave it. Let's go, M'Baku."

M'Baku looked as if he wanted to throttle Tafari, but he let out a breath and retreated. "Better watch who you're talking to," he said, brushing Tafari's shoulder as they passed.

Tafari stepped aside. "See you at the festival. Should be a lot of fun."

His friends laughed as if sharing in some kind of private joke.

T'Challa and his friends remained quiet until Tafari and his group were out of sight.

"What in the world was that all about?" Sheila asked.

T'Challa let out a stifled breath. He felt sweat run down his back. *The nerve of him! Who does he think he is?*

He waited another moment before speaking, trying his best to regain his composure. "The guy who was talking is named Tafari," he finally managed to say. "I met him at a mentorship program my father wanted me to do. When I was there, Tafari said something about Wakanda being better off before we had Vibranium. He said our true history was . . . lost to the ages."

"He needs to keep his mouth shut," M'Baku said, still bristling. "Who wants to go back to that? Wakanda was divided into tribes back then, fighting over resources and land."

"What did he whisper?" Sheila asked. "He said something in Xhosa."

M'Baku looked to the ground.

T'Challa blinked rapidly for a moment, as if embarrassed. "It means . . ."

"It means *stupid foreigner*," M'Baku said angrily. He swallowed. "Sorry."

Sheila shook her head, clearly hurt.

"Well, that's not very welcoming," Zeke said, trying to deflect the insult with humor.

But no one laughed.

"What's up with those robes?" Zeke continued. "They look like some kind of cult or something."

"Wakanda's full of cults," M'Baku said. "Like the Panther Cult."

"'Cult' has a different meaning where we come from," Sheila said. "Usually negative."

"I don't like what he said about the festival," T'Challa said.

"He said it should be fun," Zeke put in. "What's so bad about that?"

But T'Challa knew a threat when he heard one, and that was definitely Tafari's intent.

CHAPTER SEVEN

When T'Challa returned home with his friends, he did receive a few questioning looks from his guards, but that was about it. He was glad of it. The last thing he wanted to do was get into trouble while his friends were here.

He slept fitfully when night came. He was tired from the hike and mentally troubled by the encounter with Tafari and his friends.

See you at the festival. Should be a lot of fun.

What, exactly, was Tafari up to?

Should he tell his father to be on the lookout for . . . what? A bunch of kids with bad attitudes and white robes?

He turned over and punched his pillow, making a soft spot to lay his head. Was he just being paranoid? He almost laughed aloud at the thought, as he had asked himself that same question several times in the past, only to discover that his instincts for danger were usually right.

What has your prince done to earn *respect? Besides being born with a Vibranium spoon in his mouth?*

The insult still stung, and T'Challa felt it would take a while for his pride to return.

Before T'Challa met up with Zeke and Sheila the next morning, he set out early, his security detail keeping their distance a bit, as he had told them he needed some space to think.

A fine drizzle started, and T'Challa walked at a brisk pace. Vendors were setting up their stalls, offering colorful vegetables, custom-made woven baskets, beads, necklaces, and gems.

When he reached the grounds of the AYL, the drizzle had stopped, and a few early-riser students were already seated at outside tables, some reading books, others gathered together in small groups. He found Professor Silumko's lecture hall easily. He took a breath and knocked on the closed door. After a moment he heard footsteps, and then the door opened.

"Prince T'Challa," the professor greeted him. "What a pleasant surprise."

"I'm sorry to come unannounced," T'Challa replied. "And so early."

"Nonsense. Do come in. I'm afraid class won't start for an hour or so. Are you here for another visit?"

"No," T'Challa replied, "but I'd like to talk to you for a moment if you're not too busy."

Professor Silumko raised an inquisitive eyebrow and invited him in.

Instead of meeting in the lecture hall, the professor led T'Challa to a small office behind a folding screen partition, painted in the deep greens of a Wakandan forest. "Sometimes I work late," the professor said, taking stacks of papers from one place and moving them to another, "and this little room has served as a second home of sorts. Sorry for the . . . discombobulation."

T'Challa almost laughed aloud. Leave it to an academic to use a word like *discombobulation*, when *mess* would have worked just as well.

"It is quite all right," T'Challa tried to assure him. "Thank you again for seeing me without notice."

The space was cluttered with papers, books, and little decorative objects. A small window let in light. Professor Silumko moved some papers to reveal a chair and invited T'Challa to sit. "Tea?" he asked. "I have some lovely, fresh rooibos leaves. It'll only take a moment to brew a pot."

"No," T'Challa said. "Thank you. I'm fine."

Professor Silumko sat down behind a desk that looked to

be carved from a single piece of slate. He steepled his fingers and rested his elbows on the table. "So, my prince. How can I help you today?"

T'Challa shifted in his chair. Something had jabbed him. He reached under his thigh and found a small wooden carving of a panther. He held it up.

"Oh," the professor said, embarrassed. "I am so sorry. I was looking for that just the other day."

T'Challa set it on a table next to him. "Well," he finally started, "I was hoping you could tell me a bit about one of your students."

Professor Silumko tilted his head. "One of *my* students?"

"Yes. He was here when I visited. I think his name is Tafari."

The slightest twitch of a muscle jumped along the professor's jawline. He leaned back in his chair. "Ah, yes. Tafari. His family is of the Jabari Tribe. From what I understand, Tafari left his home and has not been back. I suppose he stays with friends, or has his own apartment in the city."

T'Challa found this bit of information interesting. The Jabari Tribe were isolationists and did not follow Bast or the Panther Tribe. Their deity was Hanuman, and his followers called themselves the White Gorilla Cult. They dwelled in the mountains and shunned technology and Vibranium. *Just like Tafari*, T'Challa realized.

"He is a bright student," the professor continued, "but also disruptive. I am so sorry if he offended you."

"I wasn't offended," T'Challa said, even though he had been. "What else can you tell me about him?"

The professor fiddled with another small carving on his desk, this one of a snake with green gems for eyes. "He is strong-willed. Opinionated. He could be a great leader. But I'm afraid his ideas are a little . . . radical for modern tastes."

"You mean when he was saying Wakandans were better off before Vibranium?"

"Yes, that is one of the things he has brought up in class."

T'Challa nodded. "And what else has he . . . brought up in class?"

The professor swallowed, and it seemed to T'Challa that he was nervous. Maybe it was just that he was being questioned by a member of the royal family. But T'Challa really didn't care. He wanted to know everything there was about Tafari.

Born with a Vibranium spoon in his mouth . . .

"Well," Professor Silumko began, "he thinks that we are a lost people. He once said that he often wondered who was here *before* Bast and the Orishas."

T'Challa rubbed his chin. His mother had told him stories of the Orishas when he was just a young child. They made up the pantheon of Wakanda's gods: Thoth, Kokou, Mujaji, Ptah, Nyami, and most powerful of all, Bast. These weren't just mythological names to Wakandans. They were as real as the air they breathed.

"So," T'Challa said. "Who *was* here before the Orishas? Did Tafari ever get an answer?"

Professor Silumko removed his glasses and cleaned them with a cloth from his desk. He seemed troubled, T'Challa noticed, judging by his fidgetiness.

"Some say that long ago," he started, "long before Bashenga and Bast, there were . . . others here."

"Others?" T'Challa repeated.

The professor placed his glasses back on the bridge of his nose. He paused a moment and studied T'Challa. "Today, we would call them demons. Supernatural creatures so old no one remembers their names. But they were banished to the Nether-Realms by Bast and the Orishas long ago, locked away for all eternity."

There was another moment of silence. T'Challa had never heard this before as a child. How was that possible? He tried to keep his composure and not let his ignorance of Wakandan history show.

Professor Silumko coughed slightly and shifted in his chair. "If I may ask, my prince, why the concern about Tafari?"

T'Challa hesitated. He wasn't sure what to say. "I, um, well . . . I saw him yesterday with some other students. They were dressed in white robes and acting kind of . . . strange."

Another uncomfortable twitch from the professor. "Interesting," he said. "I really have no idea what that's all about."

T'Challa nodded and rose from his seat. "Thank you, Professor. I appreciate your time."

"My pleasure, Prince T'Challa." He stood up and checked his watch. "Would you like to stay for a while? We'll be discussing moral philosophy and its relation to world religions."

"No. But thank you. I do appreciate your time."

As T'Challa left his office, he realized he now had more questions than answers.

CHAPTER EIGHT

T'Challa dreamt of the gods that night. They flashed in and out of his consciousness, all-knowing and mighty, beyond human understanding. When he woke, he thought of Professor Silumko's comment: *Today, we would call them demons. Supernatural creatures so old no one remembers their names.*

Why had he not learned of this growing up?

Had his teachers, and, more importantly, his mother and father, never told him of this hidden history?

He found it hard to believe.

Everyone knew the story of Bashenga and how Bast showed him the way to the heart-shaped herb, paving the way for the Panther Cult and its followers. But was there more to the tale? An aspect of history stripped from the official record?

T'Challa made a mental note to ask his father and mother more.

He put Tafari out of his mind and set out to see Zeke and Sheila. They all left the palace after an early breakfast, and T'Challa's first surprise for them was their means of transportation.

"We'll be using hover bikes," T'Challa told them.

"Wow!" Zeke exclaimed, running his hands along the smooth frame of one of the vehicles.

It was built on the model of a motorcycle, but unlike any Zeke and Sheila had ever seen before. There was a windscreen, slots for your feet, and handlebars. Most curious of all, there was only one wheel in the front, which made the whole machine lean forward in a dynamic, aggressive stance. The back boasted what looked like wings on either side.

Both Zeke and Sheila listened as T'Challa showed them the controls.

"There are two different speeds," he explained, "but I recommend you stick to phase one. I'll go slow to start."

Sheila looked at every detail of the bike with curiosity, the gears in her mind turning. "So, this strip along the bottom, that's where the energy conductor is, right?"

"Correct," T'Challa replied. "The tracks that run along

the city streets have superconducting magnets. One strip repels and the other attracts, lifting the bike or train from the ground."

"Awesome," Zeke said.

"Ready?" T'Challa asked.

Zeke and Sheila warily climbed on their bikes.

"Oh," T'Challa said. "One last thing. Press the red button."

Zeke and Sheila did as they were asked. Instantly, both bikes made a whirring sound and a bubble of what looked like glass enveloped their bodies, sealing them in.

"Safety first," T'Challa said, and took off.

Zeke and Sheila followed quickly, getting used to the feel and weight of the bikes.

"Amazing!" Zeke shouted, catching up to T'Challa.

"I can feel the magnets under the bike!" Sheila added.

T'Challa led them down one of the less congested city streets, Zeke and Sheila exclaiming the whole time. They leaned into curves, shifting their weight like pro racers.

"This is like a video game!" Sheila called out.

"But you don't play video games!" Zeke shouted back.

"But I *imagine* this is what it feels like!" Sheila answered.

"Get ready to slow down!" T'Challa called.

They rounded a corner and T'Challa eased his speed until they came to a stop. Zeke and Sheila followed T'Challa's lead and pressed the red button again, releasing the shields.

"This is just too cool!" Zeke said. "We need this tech in America!"

"Don't hold your breath," Sheila said. "We're still trying to get high-speed trains in every major city."

T'Challa recalled taking the elevated train in Chicago. While it was a fun experience, he did think it was a pretty slow way to travel.

"Hey," Zeke asked. "How were we able to hear each other through the glass?"

"I linked the bikes earlier," T'Challa said. "Kind of like Bluetooth, but based on Vibranium technology."

Sheila shook her head in wonderment.

"What's next?" Zeke asked.

T'Challa smiled. "Follow me."

He led them along another city street, this one a winding narrow path with storefronts crammed on either side. Zeke and Sheila took the curves and turns as well as T'Challa.

The narrow path widened and the street became less crowded. Up ahead, the sun was bright, and T'Challa put the bike in a lower speed, letting his friends catch up before finally stopping. They released the glass shields.

"Oh my," Sheila said, breathing hard.

Zeke was speechless.

Ahead of them, a brilliant blue lake shimmered, speckles of sun glinting off the water.

"This is Lake Turkana," T'Challa said.

"It's beautiful," Sheila whispered.

They set down their hover bikes and walked a short distance to the edge of the water. A few people were out enjoying the weather and the lake breezes. Seagulls, terns, and even an albatross swooped and dove for morsels of food on the beach. T'Challa took a deep breath. "I used to come here a lot a few years ago. I'd sit here for hours, looking out at the water."

"Well," Zeke said, taking off his sneakers and T-shirt. "Last one in is a rotten egg!"

Surprise dawned on T'Challa's face as Zeke sprinted off and into the water, kicking sand in his wake. He bobbed his head under and came back up sputtering. "It's crystal clear!" he shouted.

T'Challa looked at Sheila. "I don't have a swimsuit," she said.

"Well," T'Challa replied, "neither do I!"

And with that, they both took off to join Zeke, clothes and all.

T'Challa suddenly felt like a child again, splashing and laughing and trying to stand on his friends' shoulders. It was just what he needed to relax. Fortunately, none of the other beachgoers recognized him.

They came out of the water dripping wet, but the sun was so intense they were fairly dry after sitting for another half hour. T'Challa enjoyed lying in the sun, feeling the heat on his face and back. It was such a simple thing, but one that he had not experienced in quite some time. He heard his father's voice in his head, something that he had said more than once. *The time will soon come when you have to put away childish concerns, T'Challa. Remember that.*

T'Challa's tranquil mood was suddenly broken by thoughts of who he was and his destiny.

"Hey," Zeke called, shading his eyes with his hand, "when's that festival thing happening?"

T'Challa tensed. His stomach pitched as he realized that the Festival of the Ancestors was tomorrow.

See you at the festival. Should be a lot of fun.

A dark cloud passed over the sun.

CHAPTER NINE

The next evening, Wakanda was abuzz with excitement. T'Challa, along with Shuri and M'Baku, met Zeke and Sheila outside their residence. He was also surprised to see three of the Dora Milaje silently waiting, their faces stoic.

"Father says he wants them with us," Shuri whispered. "Big crowds, you know?"

T'Challa eyed the warriors carefully. They looked ready to spring into action at a moment's notice. He gave a brief smile and nod, and, in unison, they all raised their left arm in a closed fist over their hearts.

"So," T'Challa asked, "are we ready?"

"Yup," Zeke said. Sheila beamed alongside him. T'Challa was glad his father had allowed his friends to attend the festival. He was also happy to see that Shuri wasn't wearing a Bast costume, after all. She wore an electric-blue jumpsuit with plenty of pockets for her gadgets.

The Dora Milaje flanked them as they walked. T'Challa noticed that Zeke looked completely awestruck and terrified of them.

"Just look at that moon," Sheila said, peering up.

T'Challa peered skyward. The moon hung low and heavy in the sky, a fiery-red witness to the night's events.

Zeke slipped his backpack off and rummaged around inside it. "Speaking of the moon, I brought you something, T'Challa. Catch."

T'Challa raised his hands in a reflex motion. "MoonPies!" he half shouted.

"What's a MoonPie?" M'Baku asked.

T'Challa unwrapped the package and handed one of the chocolaty marshmallow treats to M'Baku, who studied it closely and then took a bite. He was quiet for a moment as he chewed, considering. "Tastes good," he finally said, staring at Zeke. "You know, you're not so bad after all. I don't care what anyone says about you."

"Right," Zeke said flatly. "Thanks."

"Hey," T'Challa said. "Look up there."

Up ahead, what seemed like a thousand fireflies winked their yellow, finger-staining light in the trees. Crowds of people were sitting on the soft ground or standing with children on their shoulders. Mount Bashenga stood high, its majestic peak soaring to the night sky, the strange red moon its backdrop.

"This is going to be excellent!" T'Challa said, but again he remembered Tafari's cryptic message. He hadn't said anything to his father. He didn't want to run to the king for every odd comment or action. That would just prove Tafari right:

You should head back to the palace. Wouldn't want your royal robes getting dirty.

T'Challa shook the troubling thoughts away. He just wanted to blend in and not draw attention to himself. His father, of course, would be making an appearance as the ruler of the nation.

Thousands of people were in attendance, a multitude of bright-colored clothing as far as the eye could see. Wakandan flags waved from every peak, and percussive music thumped from unseen speakers. T'Challa and his friends took seats on a hill overlooking the festivities.

"Here we go!" Shuri exclaimed.

Silence descended. A single bright light appeared in the eastern sky, and a deep, strong voice carried out over the crowd. "Years and years ago, when the five tribes of Wakanda were divided, a great meteor crashed from the heavens."

The solitary dot of light expanded—a ring of fire crackling around its edges—and formed into a fiery ball of flame, which soared through the sky, only to disappear in the distance, accompanied by a deafening *boom!*

"Wow!" Zeke shouted over the blast. "This is the best light show ever!"

"A meteor," the voice went on, "that would change the future of our nation."

Drums began to pound in the distance, *boom, boom, boom*, a rhythmic beat that entranced the audience.

"And from that cataclysmic event, a nation was transformed."

Zeke looked on, awestruck, as the air shimmered in front of him. Bright silver lines began to run down Mount Bashenga, sparkling in the dark, as if Vibranium itself was pouring forth from the mountain like white lava.

The unseen voice suddenly took on a dire tone.

"But all was not . . . as we might have thought. . . ."

The drumbeats became more ominous, faster and faster, *boom, boom, boom, boom*. T'Challa felt the reverberations in the soles of his feet and along his spine. Faces appeared in the sky in a spectrum of hues: sparkling red and green, blinding white, and electric blue.

"Some of our people were contaminated by the wreckage and became possessed . . ." the voice continued, "as if . . . by evil spirits."

T'Challa watched as the faces became monstrous, grotesque images that threw their heads back and howled, echoing out over the assembled masses. One small boy next to T'Challa cried out and hugged his father.

"But Bashenga, a great warrior shaman, prayed to the Panther Goddess, Bast."

A cheer went up as a massive panther took shape in the stars, like a constellation just now revealed.

"And Bast . . . answered his call!" the narrator cried out.

She heard my call, too, T'Challa thought. *Run, Young Panther. Run.*

Bast leapt in the night sky, and a tremendous roar shook the very ground upon which T'Challa and his friends sat.

The narrator continued his tale.

"Bast led Bashenga to the heart-shaped herb, giving him power beyond ordinary men."

Tall reeds and wild grass sprang up around T'Challa and his friends, waving in the night breeze. T'Challa wondered what it would have been like, thousands of years ago, to witness such an event—to be there at the beginning of Wakanda's birth. Sheila reached out to touch a gently waving reed, but her hand only grasped empty air. It was all a holographic display.

"And now," the voice went on, "today, we pay tribute to our king, a line passed down from Bashenga's generation."

A flaring bright light shone onto a stage to reveal the speaker, a man in red robes, holding a great wooden staff. "People of Wakanda!" he shouted. "I give you . . . King

T'Chaka! The Black Panther! And Queen . . . Ramonda!"

A deafening roar of applause went up through the crowd as T'Challa's parents were presented, standing on a raised dais of black stone. Shuri waved her arms in the air, and the Wakandan battle cry escaped her lips. "Yibambe! Yibambe!"

"What does it mean?" Zeke asked.

Shuri paused in her celebration. "It's a call to come together," she shouted over the din of the crowd, "but you could say it means 'hold strong'!"

"Yibambe!" Zeke shouted with renewed enthusiasm. "Yibambe!"

Sheila laughed at Zeke's excitement.

T'Challa felt pride flood his body. Queen Ramonda stood beside his father, her face fierce and proud. But it wasn't just the king and queen on the stage. Every tribal leader, elder, mystic, and shaman of the Panther Cult was there, too, as a show of strength and unity. The Dora Milaje flanked them on both sides, motionless yet alert, ready for any threat.

King T'Chaka held up his hand for quiet, which fell immediately. He didn't wear the panther suit but ceremonial clothing adorned with the Panther Tribe's colors and sigils. He looked out at the crowd, and T'Challa felt as if his father was searching for him and his sister. They could have been up there with him, all members of the royal family together, but he and Shuri had both preferred not to share in the literal spotlight. Their parents understood and had allowed them this one small bit of personal freedom.

Now T'Challa stared at both of his parents, standing tall with all of Wakanda before them.

"My people," King T'Chaka called out. "We are a strong nation, but our strength only comes through unity and peace."

The crowd applauded, cheers of support in the dark.

"We would be nothing," the king continued, "without all of us working together to make Wakanda a great nation. Our ancestors knew this, which is why we have stayed true to our creed all these years."

T'Challa felt a tingle run along his arms. At first, he thought it was just cool air, but the sensation seemed to travel up his arms and to his neck. "Strange," he whispered.

"What?" Zeke asked.

"The air," T'Challa said. "Do you feel that?"

"I thought it was some kind of outside air-conditioning," Zeke replied, rubbing his arms.

Sheila turned to the two of them. "Why's it so cold all of a sudden?"

A nervous murmuring buzzed through the crowd. Wakandan flags, placed around the festival grounds, suddenly flapped and rattled in the wind. King T'Chaka looked to the sky, as did the three Dora Milaje around T'Challa.

"What is going on?" Shuri shouted.

The wind continued to rise now, a howl growing louder and louder. T'Challa watched as people suddenly ran for the safety of enclosed places. Children began to cry at the sudden turn of the wind and weather. Alarm dawned on Sheila's and Zeke's faces.

"T'Challa?" Sheila said, her voice wavering.

"Look!" Shuri shouted.

T'Challa turned.

He didn't understand what he was seeing.

A whirling mass of some sort of white energy—almost like a whirlpool with fire around its edges—formed above the stage. A jagged black line was at the center of it, like lightning pulsating in a dark storm cloud.

T'Challa squinted. Symbols of some sort—in a language he didn't know—curled and formed in the circle, some swirling and some burning brightly as gold and then fading. T'Challa felt the circle's pull, as strong as a magnet.

The Dora Milaje snapped to attention and formed a protective ring around the king and queen, their spears ready to face whatever threat was coming.

At that moment, the circle flared.

And then something came out of it.

At first, T'Challa thought he was looking at smoke from the fireworks taking over the stage, but smoke didn't move the way this moved. This was fluid and . . . *purposeful*, as if some human force was behind it.

He stood still for a moment, shock deadening his ability to move. The ghostly forms were almost solid, like figures at the edge of a dream, hovering and waiting.

"T'Challa?" Zeke said. "What is . . ."

But T'Challa didn't hear the rest of the sentence.

He had only one thing on his mind.

His parents.

He willed his legs to move and rushed forward, ignoring the cries of Shuri and M'Baku behind him.

"Prince T'Challa!" one of the Dora Milaje shouted above the frenzy. "Stay back!"

Strong arms grabbed him and held him tight. "No!" T'Challa cried out. "Let me go!"

"We must protect you, Prince T'Challa!" another one of them said. "It is our duty!"

The swirling forms were twining themselves around T'Challa's father and mother like spiderwebs, binding them where they stood.

"Father!" T'Challa shouted with all the breath he had.

A screeching sound blasted out over the masses, a piercing, high-pitched wail. Wakandans clamped their hands over their ears and dropped to their knees. T'Challa felt his head spin. His tongue stuck to the roof of his mouth.

The Dora Milaje lunged, parried, and thrust at the shadowy creatures with their spears, but the forms didn't seem to feel the effects, and the warriors were soon overwhelmed, losing their weapons as they tried to break free with their arms and legs. The people on the stage were being sucked into that black hole of nothingness, T'Challa saw, as if it were a giant vacuum.

What in the name of Bast? he thought.

But this was not Bast. This was something different. Something ancient. Something beyond this world.

I have to stop this! he told himself.

I have to!

The screeching wail still rang in his ears, but he used every ounce of will and strength to break free from the grasp of his guards. He pushed his way through the frantic mob.

A blur flashed at the edge of his vision. It was a figure in white, running toward the stage. But before T'Challa could react, a deafening *crack* exploded in his ears, knocking him back and to the ground.

Confused voices rang out:

"Was it a bomb?"

"We're under attack!"

And as T'Challa tried to rise, he saw, just for an instant, what this strange, smokelike enemy really was. They were creatures of unfathomable appearance, both snakelike and simian, gargantuan and ferocious, with distorted faces full of malice.

The white-clad figure threw back his hood.

T'Challa knew that face.

Tafari.

"Let this day be one that is remembered!" Tafari shouted. "The day when the monarchy fell! Power to the Old Ones! Long live the Originators!"

T'Challa slumped back down to the ground.

And then everything went black.

CHAPTER
TEN

T'Chaka, the Black Panther and King of Wakanda, was missing.

Queen Ramonda was also unaccounted for, as were Wakanda's elders and several Dora Milaje.

Immediately after the attack, T'Challa, Sheila, Zeke, Shuri, and M'Baku gathered in the safety of the palace. Shuri paced the room nervously. "We have to find Father and Mother!" she cried out, for what must have been the hundredth time. "Now!"

The three Dora Milaje who were assigned to protect them were unharmed, as they hadn't gotten close enough to be caught up in whatever strange force had taken T'Challa's parents. One of them, the one with the strong arms who had held T'Challa tight, stood in front of him. "Prince T'Challa, I am Akema. These are my sisters, Cebisa and Isipho."

T'Challa's gaze roamed over the Dora Milaje. They all looked as if they were cut from the same hard rock. "We are at your service, Prince," Akema said.

T'Challa had a decision to make. His mother and father were nowhere to be seen. He had to show quick thinking and courage if he was now in command.

The sudden thought of it startled him. *I am in command.*

"Thank you, Akema," he began, determined to make a plan before the enormity of the situation completely overwhelmed him. "Check the perimeter of the palace and all the rooms. We need to make sure no one uses this crisis to do further damage. I will call on you when needed."

A tightness around Akema's mouth was the only sign of her distress. "My prince, it is our duty to be at your side now, more than ever. We must stay close."

T'Challa felt like he couldn't think. His mind was racing. He opened his mouth to speak, but Akema beat him to it. "I will remain by the door while I send Cebisa and Isipho to check that all is locked down."

She snapped her head at her sisters, a silent command. They disappeared quickly and Akema then walked to the door, spear in hand, and took up her watch.

T'Challa looked to Shuri. He could feel her pain in the pit of his stomach. He wondered if his parents were even still alive. He couldn't say it aloud, but the thought of it cast a pall over the room and left him feeling shattered. He had seen that whirling circle of emptiness as people were sucked up into it.

"Tafari!" T'Challa muttered, clenching his fist. "He will pay for this!"

Sheila and Zeke, still in shock, sat without speaking. They had come to Wakanda for a once-in-a-lifetime experience. Now they were caught in a whirlwind of terror and confusion.

"Father wasn't wearing his suit," Shuri said. "Remember? He was vulnerable!"

T'Challa laid a comforting hand on his sister's shoulder. He tried to calm his mind and focus. That was what his father always told him:

Nothing is ever accomplished through anger.

"How could they have done it?" M'Baku asked. "What kind of weapon was it?"

"It wasn't a weapon," T'Challa said. He remembered what he saw before he became unconscious: terrible faces and nightmarish forms, hungry to destroy anything in their path. "I saw them. They were . . . creatures of some sort. They came out of that portal . . . or whatever it was."

"Creatures?" Zeke ventured, and his face showed his distress. "Not again."

"How could this . . . Tafari be in league with monsters?" Sheila asked.

"His professor," T'Challa said, "a man named Silumko, said that Tafari was interested in Wakanda's past. He wanted to know who was here *before* Bast and the Orishas."

"'Power to the Old Ones,'" Shuri whispered. "'Long live the Originators.' That's what he said. Who are the Originators?"

And that's when T'Challa remembered. It was something that Professor Silumko had said when he had visited the AYL:

Today, we would call them demons. Supernatural creatures so old no one remembers their names.

Was that who these Originators were?

T'Challa was stunned. Could Tafari have called upon these creatures? How?

"I knew that dude was up to no good," M'Baku said, his voice as sharp as a knife's edge. "My parents were up there on that stage, too. They're gone!" He put his head in his hands. His father, N'Gamo, sat on the Black Panther's war council, and his mother was a high-ranking official in the royal court.

"We will get them back," T'Challa tried to reassure him. "I promise you."

M'Baku wiped a tear from his cheek.

"That sound," Zeke said, rubbing his ear. "That high-pitched ringing. What was it?"

"Felt like some kind of psionic attack," Shuri said.

"Psionic?" M'Baku managed to ask.

"It's, like, using a psychic ability to create damage," Shuri explained. "Like a telepath, someone who can get inside your mind or something."

Zeke lowered his head to his knees.

They all sat for a moment without speaking. T'Challa felt empty and devastated. It must have been one a.m. at this point. Shuri finally broke the silence, and when she spoke, T'Challa was glad to hear her voice was calm. "You have to do something, T'Challa. Talk to the nation. They need to see a leader."

Shuri was right, T'Challa knew. He had to show the people a symbol of hope. At this moment, he was the leader of Wakanda. The sudden clarity of it sent a shock of adrenaline through his body, and he once again heard his father's voice in his head.

You must be ready to lead when the time comes, son.

But I'm not ready yet, T'Challa told himself. *Am I?*

Before he could think on it any longer, his Kimoyo Bracelet pulsed, a sign of an incoming message. But he wasn't the only one to receive it. Shuri's bracelet pulsed as well.

"What the . . . ?" Shuri started. "Who's sending this?"

Akema turned from her station at the door and rushed to join them. "A message?" she asked, her voice hopeful.

T'Challa nodded and then took a breath. He looked at Shuri and tapped the bead on his wrist. There was a flash of static for a moment, and then a familiar face materialized in a 3D hologram. It was Tafari. And he wasn't alone. His white-robed companions were behind him in a triangle formation, with Tafari at the apex. T'Challa couldn't make out exactly where they were, but it looked like a dark room of some sort, with no identifiable features. Tafari was the only one to have his hood thrown back, revealing his smug, self-satisfied face.

"What have you done?" T'Challa demanded before Tafari had a chance to speak. "Where are my parents?"

"They are beyond time and space," a voice said, and one of the white-robed figures pulled back his hood, revealing another familiar face.

T'Challa gasped. "Professor Silumko?"

"It is not just your parents, T'Challa," the professor said. "It is every shaman, elder, and government official who holds power in Wakanda."

"Who will protect the nation now that the mighty Black Panther is gone?" Tafari said. "The monarchy is over. It is time for new gods to rule. The *real* gods. And I will be their high priest."

"You're out of your mind!" M'Baku shouted.

"You will pay for this!" Shuri snapped. "All of you!"

"Hush now, Princess," Tafari said in a condescending tone.

Shuri's eyes brimmed with tears and rage.

"We are the future," Tafari said, holding up his hands. A serpentine ring circled one finger. "It is time for a new generation, one untethered from the curse of Vibranium and all the turmoil it has brought."

T'Challa felt his blood boiling. He unconsciously clenched his fists.

"You see," Tafari went on, "for generations, Wakandans have worshipped at the feet of Bast. But Bast is a usurper, a false idol." He paused. "Like your father."

Akema actually hissed in anger.

T'Challa closed his eyes and opened them again. He tried to steady his breathing and then spoke slowly. "I ask you once again. Where are Wakanda's leaders?"

"They have been banished," Professor Silumko said.

"Banished?" Shuri repeated. "Banished where?"

"To a place from which they will never return," Tafari replied. He leaned in, so that his image was closer to T'Challa. "But you, T'Challa and Shuri, you have a chance to help show our young people the true path. That is why . . . *they* allowed the young to remain unharmed. It is our chance to prove our worth." He paused and raised his head higher, as if speaking to those he thought beneath him. "So, I ask you: Are you with me, or will you continue to worship the false gods of your parents?"

T'Challa looked to his sister, who slowly shook her head in refusal. There was no way he was giving in to this. "I reject your proposal," he declared. "This is treason. And when I find my mother and father, you will all be held accountable!"

Zeke and Sheila watched him with pride. This was the T'Challa they knew, one not afraid to stand up to bullies and those who would do harm.

"So be it," Tafari said. "Don't say I didn't offer you a way out."

There was a moment of silence. T'Challa could hear his own heartbeat pounding in his chest.

"We will be watching," Tafari continued, "and I promise you, Young Panther, we will return."

The screen went dark.

CHAPTER ELEVEN

T'Challa left the palace, Akema and her sisters a few steps behind him. Zeke and Sheila had tried to accompany him, but he had refused. Now he stood where the Festival of the Ancestors had taken place. The stage was destroyed, and debris littered the area. Torn banners and flags lay fluttering in the breeze.

His eyes suddenly filled with tears.

Who will protect the nation now that the mighty Black Panther is gone?

He should have said something, he scolded himself—told his father that he suspected an attack.

See you at the festival. Should be a lot of fun.

He knew he should have taken Tafari's threat more seriously.

Another lesson learned, he told himself.

His mind raced with questions. Professor Silumko said his parents were in a place beyond time and space. *Where could that be?*

The Originators.

How had Tafari called them here, if that was truly what he had done?

He saw the strange entities in his mind's eye. They were real. There was no doubt about it. Now he had to figure out a way to defeat them and get his parents back.

He struggled on what to do.

Every scenario that ran through his mind seemed foolish.

Footsteps sounded behind him and he spun around, fists clenched.

"Prince," Akema said.

T'Challa relaxed his shoulders.

"I am sorry to disturb you," she went on, "but I need to learn more of these intruders. Tell me everything you know."

T'Challa looked to the ground for a moment and then raised his head. Akema was tall, like most of the Dora Milaje, and her limbs were lean and muscled. A black cuff circled her left bicep. He met her eyes, a brilliant, luminous green.

"I know as much as you do," he said. "What you heard back there. At the palace. Tafari is a boy from the AYL who does not follow Bast."

Akema's eyes flickered, as if she were physically wounded.

"He has followers who believe Wakanda was better off in the past," T'Challa finished.

"We will find them," Akema said. "The king and queen."

T'Challa wanted the same thing. But he had no idea how to do it.

Back at the palace, he found Shuri and the others wearing glum faces. Akema and her sisters took up residence in the apartment next to his, close enough to come if needed, but also to give the prince and princess their privacy.

Zeke and Sheila still seemed in shock, and sat without speaking.

"Shuri's right," T'Challa said suddenly. "I have to address the nation."

"Good," Shuri said.

T'Challa inhaled and then tapped a bead on his Kimoyo Bracelet.

No response.

He tried it again with the same result.

"Shuri," he called. "M'Baku. Try yours."

Both Shuri and M'Baku tried to get a connection, but nothing worked.

T'Challa bit his lip. He walked to an area in the throne room that displayed a row of monitors built into the black onyx wall. He swiped his finger across the blank screen, which remained a glossy black. "Nothing," he said. "Wakanda is without communication."

"Oh, man," Zeke groaned.

"Tafari must have disabled it after his initial message to us," M'Baku suggested.

"If he wants to return to the old ways," Sheila said, "then technology would be something he'd want to get rid of."

"I think you're right, Sheila," Shuri said.

"How could he have shut down the whole Wakandan network?" M'Baku put in.

"I'll look into it," Shuri replied. She turned to Sheila. "T'Challa says you're good with computers?"

Sheila nodded.

"We'll work together, then," Shuri told her.

Even in the midst of the tragedy, T'Challa could sense Sheila's heart swell.

"We may not have the network up," T'Challa said, "but there *is* another way to get a message out. M'Baku and Shuri, head out tomorrow morning and speak to the people you see. Tell them that the prince will speak to them here at the Royal Palace, at noon. Spread the word as far as you can."

"Tomorrow?" Shuri challenged him. "We have to do something now, T'Challa! Mother and Father wouldn't want us to wait!"

T'Challa looked his sister in the eye. "We have to rest, Shuri. You'll need your stamina tomorrow morning. A cloudy mind brings no rain."

Shuri swallowed. Her lip trembled. "That's what she always says. Mother."

T'Challa looked at his friends and sister. They were all exhausted, terrified, and at a loss for answers.

"What are you going to do?" M'Baku asked.

"I'm going to figure out what to say," T'Challa replied. He immediately turned to Zeke and Sheila. He exhaled a deep sigh, as if he were carrying the weight of the world upon his shoulders. "Looks like you're here at a very unfortunate time, guys." He paused and wrung his hands, searching for the right words. "I think it would probably be best if you got on a plane back home."

Sheila's and Zeke's faces both told the same story: shock and disbelief.

"No way we're bailing out now," Zeke said.

"You know we always stick together, T'Challa," Sheila added. "Through thick and thin."

"I just want to be careful," T'Challa replied. "I don't want anything to happen to you guys, and I have no idea what's to come or what we're getting into."

"And we don't know what's coming, either," Sheila said. "Hasn't stopped us before."

Zeke nodded along. "You know what we always say, right?"

"One for all . . ." Sheila said.

T'Challa managed a smile. "And all for one."

CHAPTER
TWELVE

T'Challa stayed in the throne room a long time that evening. Sheila and Zeke were in their respective quarters, and M'Baku left to check on his neighbors. Akema stood outside the throne room door. Even when T'Challa told her to retire, she did not.

He ran his fingers along the armrests of his father's seat. The black onyx was cold to the touch. He thought for a moment of sitting in it but decided against it. He imagined his father there, strong and proud, the voices of Black Panthers long past guiding him.

Bast, show me the way.

The voice in the back of his mind was persistent. One

part of him was committed to remaining calm and finding an answer through strategy and careful thinking. The other part wanted him to pick up a spear and search for his parents. It was a constant battle he waged in his own mind.

Tafari had called Bast a usurper. That was blasphemy to T'Challa's thinking, and would surely be to other Wakandans as well.

He wasn't even sure what he would say to his people tomorrow. But he had to say something. He was the son of the Black Panther, and his voice needed to be heard. He recalled something his mother had told him not too long ago:

Sometimes there are threats even from within.

"Brother," Shuri said, closing the door behind her. "I couldn't sleep either." She took a seat in one of the chairs usually reserved for visitors.

T'Challa rubbed his brow.

"It's okay, big bro. We're all . . . out of sorts."

"Where could they be?" T'Challa asked.

"'Beyond time and space' is what that professor dude said."

The idea of it almost sent T'Challa into a sort of panic.

"What, exactly, does that mean?" he asked.

"I'm not sure yet," Shuri replied. "If Tafari did bring creatures here from the past, that means he's in possession of some serious and powerful magic. Where could he have gotten it?"

"We'll find out," T'Challa said, although he didn't have the slightest clue how.

Sunrise in Wakanda brought hundreds to the Royal Palace grounds. The nation was represented, but there were no elders or people in positions of power, only Wakandans who worked hard every day to see their nation thrive.

T'Challa was tired and stressed; his sleep had been nothing but a sequence of startling imagery. He needed to focus but was having a tough time of it.

A troubling thought suddenly came to the forefront of his mind. If another nation knew of Wakanda's weakness, they could surely use it to their advantage. The Great Mound could be exploited.

I can't let that happen, he told himself. *Not ever.*

The people gathered at the palace all told conflicting stories. Some said it was an invasion from creatures called the Chitauri, a militaristic, space-faring species with an appetite for war. But they all agreed on one thing. Their leader, their fierce warrior, the Black Panther, was nowhere to be seen. He and the queen and every other official were swept up in "the Event," as people began to call it.

It was a calculated strike.

T'Challa's nerves were on edge as he looked out at the crowd. Shuri and M'Baku had been successful in spreading the word. People talked among themselves, wondering what was to come. T'Challa and Shuri stood in front of a giant monument to Bast, carved from an enormous piece of coal-black onyx. Sheila, Zeke, and M'Baku were in the first row near the stage. Akema, Cebisa, and Isipho scanned the crowd for threats. *The Dora Milaje need to be seen with me,* he thought. *A show of security, not anarchy.*

T'Challa felt a slight breeze on his face, and for that he was grateful. He didn't want people to see him sweating with anxiety. Shuri was beside him, and together, they formed a united front.

T'Challa's eye was drawn to a group of young people standing apart from the others, whispering conspiratorially, he thought, to each other. What were they saying? Who were they? More of Tafari's followers?

He turned away, facing front. "People of Wakanda," he started, and he was glad that his voice didn't crack. "Our nation—*your* nation—was attacked. My father and mother, your king and queen, are missing." He paused and swallowed. Shuri gave him a reassuring look. "My sister and I will do everything we can to return your loved ones safely to our country . . . and bring their attackers to heel."

The crowd was silent. It seemed to him that his words were falling on deaf ears. They needed a leader, not someone shouting empty words of hope. He swallowed the lump in his throat. "These . . . traitors will pay for what they have done."

"Perhaps they are not traitors," a voice called. "Perhaps they just want change."

T'Challa turned the same time Akema did, looking for the voice that had rung out. He scanned the crowd again. A young man raised his head when T'Challa's eyes fell on him. He was one of the ones T'Challa had spotted earlier.

"Maybe Wakanda deserves this," the protestor continued. "Maybe we should not bow down to one man, a king who craves and clings to power."

T'Challa saw Akema tighten her grip on her spear.

Several people nearby shook their heads at the lone dissenter, as if he were an unruly student speaking out of turn. One man, whose arms rippled with muscle beneath his battle armor, looked as if he were about to leap into action. T'Challa held up a hand. "He has a right to be heard, as do all of you. We are all Wakandans."

Several in the audience nodded in agreement. The man finally huffed and walked away, followed by a few others. T'Challa knew there might be those who had no love for the king and the royal family. But that was their right. And a civilized nation could not stifle free speech.

T'Challa let the moment pass. He looked to Shuri, who nodded encouragingly. "As you know by now," he continued, "we are without our network of communication. This affects everything—from travel in the city to everyday necessities. We have to be careful. Check in on our elders. Share your food and water if you can."

T'Challa looked out at his people. He saw their faces: hopeful, uncertain, sad. "I promise you, we will not fail."

Shuri crossed her arms on her chest. "Wakanda forever!" she shouted.

The call hung and echoed in the air for what seemed an eternity. A Wakandan flag, still on the ground from the night before, stirred in the air and flew away. T'Challa swallowed nervously. He looked to his sister and then back to the crowd. "Wakanda forever!" he echoed her.

Silence filled the air.

His heart fell. He couldn't even rally his people for a call and response.

"Wakanda forever!" a woman's single voice cried out.

T'Challa lifted his head, hopeful.

"Wakanda forever!" a man's call joined hers, loud and clear.

And then the nation shouted as one, giving T'Challa the encouragement and unity he needed.

"Wakanda forever!"

"Wakanda forever!"

"Wakanda *forever*!"

T'Challa left the stage with a sense of peace. He was glad that he and his sister had addressed the nation. He hoped it was a comfort of sorts. Now all he had to do was deliver on what he had promised.

Back in the residence, T'Challa, Shuri, and his friends remained stoic. "So," T'Challa started, "not the best time for a vacation, huh?" He tried to smile, but it just wasn't in him.

"We need a plan, T'Challa," Sheila said. "We've been through some really strange and difficult stuff before, but this . . ."

"I know," T'Challa replied. "I'm trying to keep it together. Without the Wakandan network we can't even look for clues." He turned to Shuri. "I thought you and Sheila were going to work on getting the network back up."

"We are," Shuri answered. "But no luck yet. We'll keep at it, though."

"Good," T'Challa said. He stood up and began to slowly pace around the room. "We know Tafari called those creatures here. He had to have used some kind of magic."

"But from where?" Zeke asked.

"Maybe it was a portal," Sheila suggested. "Those monsters had to get here somehow."

"Yeah!" Zeke said. "Just like in all the stories. There's always some kind of door or something."

T'Challa racked his brain for anything he had ever heard that involved some kind of dimensional travel. He absently reached to tap his Kimoyo Bracelet but then stopped and shook his head. No network. He didn't want to, but he thought of Tafari. Perhaps Wakandans *did* rely too much on technology.

"You know," Sheila said, "we need to do this the old-school way."

"And what is that?" Zeke asked.

"Before computers and advanced tech," Sheila went on, "people still figured things out, right?"

"True," T'Challa replied, wondering what his friend was getting at.

"And where did they do that?" Sheila pressed him.

T'Challa raised both hands, palms up, drawing a blank.

"The library!" Zeke shouted, jumping out of his chair.

Sheila smiled. "Exactly."

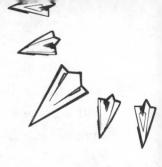

CHAPTER
THIRTEEN

It was called the Royal Library, and it was one of Wakanda's oldest treasures. T'Challa couldn't believe he hadn't thought of it earlier. It was said to rival the library of Alexandria in its wealth of information, spanning back eons. T'Challa once again wondered if Tafari had a point. Wakandan society and the world in general relied on technology so much he had forgotten that there was another way to discover information. But Tafari had chosen the wrong path to get his message across. *It's too late for him now,* T'Challa thought. *He will pay for what he has done.*

Zeke and Sheila followed T'Challa as he led them away

from their residence. He thought it important that the palace still be seen as secure, so he commanded—or, more appropriately, *asked*—Akema to remain there, outside the gates, as a symbol of strength.

The streets were quiet, even though it was only afternoon. The Royal Palace grounds housed several buildings and structures, all for different departments of Wakandan society. Amidst the temples and places of worship were buildings dedicated to arts and culture, science and engineering, transportation, economics, and more. The library lay at the far end of one block, situated between statues of Black Panthers of the past.

"There it is," T'Challa said.

The building itself was shaped like an octagon, with wide windows spanning its circumference. The glass dome atop it let in sunlight. Wakandan flags ringed the dome to be seen from every angle.

Zeke stared in wonder. "I've been to the Capitol in DC on a class trip, but this is so different from what you'd see in America."

"Got that right," Sheila said.

It was true. Wakandan architecture did not draw inspiration from Rome and Greece like so many structures around the modern world. These building had a futuristic but natural influence. There was metal, steel, and wood, sculpted into pyramids, heptagons, and circles. Decorative tiles were more common than plain bricks. Minarets hundreds of feet tall seemed to reach to the sky. One building was shaped like a wave in motion.

A set of white marble steps six feet wide led up to the double doors of the library. T'Challa pulled with both hands and they opened with a groan.

Books were lined up on shelves as far as the eye could see. Just like an American library, there were sections with different areas of interest, although the signs were not in English but in Xhosa. The relief molding that ran along the top displayed Wakandan history in a 3D-type effect: from Bast and Bashenga to silhouettes of those who once wore the mantle of Black Panther.

"Books," Zeke said reverently. "So many . . . books. It's a nerd paradise."

"I could spend hours in here," Sheila whispered.

"You just might," T'Challa said.

And they did. For the next several hours, the trio looked for anything having to do with the term *Originators*.

Zeke turned the pages of a massive volume called *Wakanda: Guiding Principles of the Past*, but came up blank.

T'Challa racked his brain for anything that could give them a clue. He tried to recall every story his mother and father had told him about Wakanda's history from the time he was a child.

"Wait," he said.

Zeke and Sheila stared with tired eyes, their expressions hopeful.

"Tafari said something else that night. . . . When the attack . . ." He trailed off. "Shuri was the one who first remembered. Tafari said, 'Power to the Old Ones. Long live the Originators.'"

"Old Ones," Zeke whispered.

T'Challa stood up and walked to a shelf. He cocked his head sideways to read the spines. After a moment, he came back to the table with a massive tome. He blew dust off the cover. Zeke sneezed.

"Looks like no one's checked that out in a while," Sheila said.

T'Challa set the book down on the table. The cover read *Tales from the Elder Days*.

"My father used to read this to me when I was a kid," he said, opening the book. "He said Wakanda had more stories than anyone could ever imagine."

"Let's hope the one we're looking for is in there," Zeke said.

T'Challa began to read.

Zeke laid his head on the table. Sheila's eyes were heavy-lidded, and her head dipped several times, only to snap back up quickly. The stress of the Event and jet lag were taking their toll.

T'Challa turned the pages slowly, his breathing loud in the quiet space. Sunlight shone down from the ceiling, revealing dust motes hanging in the air. He read. And read. And read some more, but no answers were revealed. He closed the book with a thud, causing Zeke to jump in his seat. "No luck?" Zeke asked, yawning.

T'Challa shook his head. He tried to recall his conversation with Professor Silumko and how he'd talked about Tafari's interest in Wakanda's past. Tafari had called Bast a usurper.

"Bast," T'Challa whispered.

"Huh?" Zeke said.

T'Challa stood up and walked to another narrow aisle. "I'm going to try this other room," he said. "I think there are some old, archival texts in there."

Zeke and Sheila both nodded.

T'Challa walked down the hall and around a corner. When he was a kid, he'd always wanted to see one particular room, but he never got the chance. It was full of old drawings and paintings, poems, stories, and songs. His father never let him visit, much to young T'Challa's annoyance. He had told him the artifacts stored there were too old to be handled. Now T'Challa finally had a chance to see what secrets it held.

He continued walking until he came to the familiar door. He had a fleeting memory from childhood: walking down the hall with his father, reaching up and tugging on his hand, begging to venture inside. His eyes suddenly stung.

A plaque on the door read PLEASE ASK FOR ASSISTANCE.

"Please don't be locked," T'Challa whispered.

He pushed on the door.

And it opened.

T'Challa stepped in and peered around. The smell of old paper and dust filled his nostrils. There was only one window, with a curtain drawn across it. T'Challa stood on his tiptoes and pulled it aside, letting in dim light through the frosted glass. Ladders ran along the floor, reaching all the way up to the high ceiling.

He began the hunt, searching every aisle.

He searched.

And he searched.

He wasn't sure what he was looking for, but he felt as if an answer was in here somewhere. There had to be. He recalled Professor Silumko's words:

Today, we would call them demons. Supernatural creatures so old no one remembers their names. But they were banished to the Nether-Realms by Bast and the Orishas long ago, locked away for all eternity.

If that were true, T'Challa mused, there'd have to be a record of it somewhere.

T'Challa walked farther into the room and spied a narrow hallway on his left. He made his way through to find a small table and long tubes stacked on shelves like cords of firewood. On the end of each tube's cap, stamped letters stood out along with a code of some sort. It was a system that only the librarians knew, he imagined. A box of white gloves sat nearby.

T'Challa pulled the cap from one of them, put on the white gloves, and then reached inside. Carefully, he withdrew a rolled parchment and set it on the table. He uncurled one of the pages, and what he found was fascinating beyond belief. Here was a document all about the flora and fauna of Wakanda and how it changed after the Vibranium meteor crashed to earth. Highly detailed drawings accompanied the text. Another showed animals that were now extinct. Most impressive was a species of gorilla that stood at least ten feet tall. T'Challa's head spun. *If Sheila and Zeke saw this place, they'd never leave.*

He looked for an hour until he came to a tube marked *ORI-WAK480.*

"Ori?" he whispered.

WAK surely meant Wakanda. As for 480, he hadn't a clue.

He looked up to the ceiling, musing on the letters *ORI* and what they could be an abbreviation for. "Ori . . . Orisha?"

With hands that almost shook, T'Challa pulled the tube out and unfurled the parchment.

His eyes lit up.

CHAPTER
FOURTEEN

"Cool gloves," Zeke said, rubbing his eyes.

"What'd you find?" Sheila asked.

"These pages are marked as *The Origins of the Orisha*," T'Challa replied, holding a sheaf of papers in his hands.

"Those are Wakanda's gods, right?" Sheila ventured.

"Yes," T'Challa answered. "Not just for us, but for many nations."

Zeke and Sheila sat up a little straighter.

T'Challa took a seat and carefully unrolled the first sheet of parchment. He used two small books to hold down the corners of the pages to keep them from curling. They probably hadn't been unrolled in decades. "'The Days of Pain,'" he read.

And there in the Royal Palace of Wakanda, with sunlight spilling down from the skylight, T'Challa began to read:

"'Long ago, when the plains and deserts were bare, the first people came into the land that we now call Wakanda. The air and land were dry, but the people prayed to the gods for rain, and rain did come.

"'Many an age passed, and the people came to love their land and her bounty. Dry lands bloomed with fertile, rich soil. The rivers and lakes gave forth the sustenance of fish and shell and salt.

"'But a day came when the sun dimmed and the moon burned red.

"'The mountains shook and the rivers bled.

"'And then they came.

"'They came with a great peal of thunder.

"'And the people cried out in dismay.

"'They called them the Old Ones.'"

T'Challa paused and raised his head.

Sheila and Zeke, no longer tired but energized by the tale, sat upright, eager for more.

"This is them," Sheila said. "'Power to the Old Ones.'"

"The Originators," Zeke added.

"And they came under a red moon," Sheila said. "Just like on the night of the festival."

T'Challa recalled the Wakandan moon that night. It had been bloodred. He felt a chill along his shoulders. He took a breath and continued.

"'The Old Ones were unbearable to look upon and fearsome in their visage: horned, gilled, and feathered; beaked, clawed, and fork-tongued.

"'They came upon the first people in great numbers. They were slavers and torturers, and used them to build their temples. Many were slain and the people cried out for help.

"'But there were those who stood against the Old Ones, people brave of spirit and strength, who could not be cowed. The people followed them and rallied to their call.

"'And the day came when they drove the Old Ones back.

"'The people celebrated and worshipped those fearless leaders, falling to their knees and singing their names.

"'And soon, a great and mysterious moment came.

"'The valiant ones were physically transformed by the love and power of those who followed them. They became gods, and the people called them the Orishas:

"'Nyami, the Sky Father; Thoth, with strength beyond a thousand men; Ptah, the Shaper; Mujaji, She Who Gave Us Our Name; Kokou, God of War; and above all, Bast, who dwelled in the mountaintop city of Bastet, where her followers and descendants were blessed with divine transformation.

"'The Orishas defeated and banished the Old Ones, and locked them in the Nether-Realms, beyond time and—'"

T'Challa stopped. He looked at Zeke and Sheila, and then back down at the page—

"'. . . space . . . where they remain to this day, bound and chained.'"

A moment of silence filled the library.

T'Challa swallowed. His mouth was dry. "Beyond time and space. That's where Silumko said my mother and father were."

"The Nether-Realms," Sheila said.

"And how do we get to these Nether-Realms?" Zeke asked. "And once we do, how do we—"

"We'll find a way," T'Challa said, cutting him off. "We have to."

CHAPTER
FIFTEEN

The day's revelations were still running through T'Challa's mind the next morning. The Nether-Realms. What kind of place was that? How did one get there?

He had heard plenty of fantastical tales as a child, but never one as spellbinding as the one he had read last night. He knew Wakanda hadn't just appeared out of thin air, but he knew nothing of the Old Ones and how they once inhabited the land.

His people had been enslaved.

T'Challa closed his eyes and said a silent prayer for his fallen ancestors.

He had barely slept, and spent much of the night staring at the ceiling. The whole while, a line from the text ran through his head:

The Orishas defeated and banished the Old Ones, and locked them in the Nether-Realms, beyond time and space.

How? T'Challa asked himself again. *How did Tafari and Silumko do this?*

After meeting up with Zeke and Sheila, T'Challa brought Shuri and M'Baku up to speed on their discovery. Shuri's eyes went wide with disbelief. "Our history started with Bast," she said, almost defiant, "and how she guided Bashenga to the heart-shaped herb. I've never heard any of this before!"

Sheila shook her head. "This all sounds familiar," she started. "In the States, history is sometimes neglected, and even altered to fit an agenda."

"Seems like it happens here, too," T'Challa said. He sighed. "But we have to find out where these Nether-Realms are and how to get there."

"And we don't have a lot of time," M'Baku reminded them all. "Tafari said he would be watching. Remember?"

"And that he would return," Shuri added. "When, exactly, will that be?"

T'Challa didn't know. He was exhausted. Shuri and M'Baku were right. Tafari's vague threat was still a threat. Perhaps even more dangerous because he hadn't said more.

"I don't know," T'Challa replied. "But we have to act as if whatever he has planned can come at any moment." He paused. "Shuri, any news on the network?"

Shuri scowled. "No such luck. I looked into every possible scenario, and I'm not sure how it was knocked out. Sheila thinks it was some kind of electromagnetic pulse."

T'Challa remembered the strange sensation the night of the celebration, when he'd felt a static charge run along his arms.

"Is there anything we can do to fix it?" T'Challa asked, turning to Sheila.

Sheila shook her head, frustrated. "It's beyond my skills, T'Challa. Whoever Tafari used to attack the network really knows their stuff."

"Of course," T'Challa said sarcastically. "The students at the Academy, and probably the ones in Tafari's cult, are some of the best young minds in Wakanda."

"And now they've been led astray," Shuri put in, "all under the spell of a megalomaniac."

"If these Nether-Realms are beyond time and space," Sheila said, "that means they're not on this physical plane."

T'Challa knew this in the back of his head but hadn't said it aloud yet.

"And how do you leave this physical plane?" Zeke asked.

T'Challa looked at his friend, his face serious. "There's only one way to do that, as far as I know."

Shuri raised a cautious eyebrow at her brother. "T'Challa," she said quietly. "You can't."

"What's going on?" Zeke said, looking at T'Challa and Shuri. "Can't what? How do you leave this . . . physical plane?"

"By taking the heart-shaped herb," T'Challa replied.

Zeke and Sheila exchanged wary looks.

Shuri blinked rapidly. "T'Challa. Travel to the Ancestral Plane is meant only for those about to become the Black Panther. It's a sacred act."

T'Challa recalled his history, and how Vibranium had infused the flora and fauna of Wakanda when the meteor crashed to earth all those centuries ago. The most unique of these plants was called the heart-shaped herb, a flower that, once distilled into liquid, allowed one to enter another realm. It was called the Djalia, also known as the Ancestral Plane. That was where those who would wear the mantle of the Black Panther traveled to seek the advice and wisdom of the elders. T'Challa's father had never spoken to him about his experience in the otherworld in detail, simply saying it was a personal journey meant only for him.

Zeke's voice brought him back to the moment. "Maybe he can just take a little. You know, a spoonful?"

"There is another way," a voice called.

T'Challa turned to see Akema standing in the doorway.

CHAPTER SIXTEEN

"So you were listening all this time?" T'Challa asked.

Akema came farther into the room.

"We Dora Milaje always watch," she replied. "And listen."

T'Challa wasn't sure how he felt about Akema eavesdropping. The Dora Milaje were not usually advisors to the king, only warriors. Still, he thought, this was not an ordinary time. He would expect her to be breaking protocol in his and Shuri's defense.

"Forgive me, Prince," Akema started, "but your sister is right. I have served your father for many years and have heard much. The heart-shaped herb is sacred. You are in line to rule, but not yet."

"There's another thing, too," Shuri said.

T'Challa looked to his sister, whose face was pained. "Taking it means that we are giving up. That Father isn't coming back. I, for one, won't believe that." She lowered her head.

T'Challa knew they were both right. He had to face the truth. "So," he said, trying to adopt a tone of voice that was at once commanding yet casual, "what would you advise, Akema? What is this other way you speak of?"

Akema swallowed. "May I sit, Prince?"

"Of course," T'Challa said.

Akema rested her spear in the corner and came to sit in one of the chairs. Her legs were too long for it, and she seemed out of place. A flicker of annoyance passed over her face and then disappeared. Zeke and Sheila tried to conceal their stares.

"There is a man," Akema began. "He is old now, and has been in Wakanda for as long as anyone can remember. Your mother and father sought his counsel once."

T'Challa cocked his head. "Who is this man? What is his name?"

"He is called Zawavari."

"Zawavari," T'Challa whispered.

"What does he do?" Shuri asked. "Why did Mother and Father seek him out?"

"That I do not know, Princess. I only know that we accompanied the king and queen to his domain long ago. I do not know what transpired."

T'Challa shook his head. "But what can you tell us of him, then? You said there was another way instead of taking the herb."

For the first time, T'Challa thought he saw fear in Akema's green eyes. "He is a shaman. A powerful one. It is said that he can walk among the dead."

Zeke gulped.

"Maybe he can guide you to the ancestors," Akema finished.

T'Challa looked at his sister and then at his friends. He turned to Akema. "Do you think it wise to seek him out?"

"I can only give you this knowledge, Prince. That is all."

T'Challa leaned back in his chair. "Where is he? Where is this domain you speak of?"

Akema stared at him for only a moment, but to T'Challa it felt like a lifetime.

"He resides in the Necropolis."

A moment of silence descended.

"What is . . . the Necropolis?" Sheila asked, her voice apprehensive.

"It's the place where Black Panthers of the past rest," M'Baku said. "We call it the City of the Dead."

Zeke looked as if he wanted to disappear.

"And Mother and Father told us to never play there when

we were little," Shuri added. "She said we shouldn't . . . disturb the dead."

"But this isn't playtime, Shuri," T'Challa said. "There's no other choice. If our parents and people are stuck beyond time and space, talking to this . . . Zawavari might be a way to reach them."

He turned to Akema, and this time, his voice was a command.

"Take me to him."

CHAPTER
SEVENTEEN

"But I should go, too," Shuri complained.

"I'm sorry, sister," T'Challa consoled her. "A member of the royal family needs to stay here in the palace. The people still need to know there is order."

"Even if there really isn't," Shuri huffed.

T'Challa laid a hand on her shoulder. "We'll be back before you know it. Stay strong, sister."

Shuri nodded reluctantly.

Akema insisted that only she accompany T'Challa to the Necropolis, but he refused. "Zeke, Sheila, and M'Baku are my friends," he said, "and they'd probably just follow us anyway."

Akema's fierce gaze landed on T'Challa's friends. "Do as I say. If I say to run or take shelter, do so immediately."

M'Baku nodded but Zeke and Sheila both gulped.

"What would we have to run from?" Zeke whispered, but no one replied.

They set out early the next morning after a fitful night of sleep, during which T'Challa tossed and turned for what seemed like hours. His mind was muddled and riddled with questions. But if he could get answers by talking to Zawavari, he had to do it.

Before he went to gather the others, he sought out his father's quarters. This room was not the king and queen's chambers, but a private place for the King of Wakanda only, an oasis away from the demands of running the nation. T'Challa had never entered it before. Now he stood in his father's personal space and peered around. He knew he was snooping, but this was more than simple curiosity. He needed to see if there was anything here that could help him in his quest to free his parents. *He would understand,* T'Challa told himself. *I know he would.*

It was a simple room, and no signs of overindulgence were visible. Everything seemed to be either black or gray, including the platform bed and bedding. A painting of the Wakandan skyline was the only glimmer of color. There were two well-made and sturdy chairs, unadorned but for the brass studs that dotted the leather armrests. A heavy armoire stood at the far end of the room. T'Challa approached it hesitantly.

After a moment, and a silent prayer to Bast, he pulled the doors wide.

The suit of the Black Panther hung suspended in midair, arms and legs wide apart. There were no visible wires or hangers, and it seemed to float on its own. He had no idea how it worked. "Shuri would know," he whispered aloud.

Father should have worn the suit, T'Challa thought. *Maybe it would have given him some sort of protection.*

Behind the suit, a row of shelves protruded from the wall. There were a few books, a bowl of Kimoyo beads, and a Vibranium ring.

T'Challa pulled open a drawer. A black knife with a cruel edge lay embedded in soft black velvet. The scowling face of a great ape, fangs bared, was inlaid on the hilt, which T'Challa found strange. "Hmpf," he whispered. "Never seen this before."

He lifted it out and, very carefully, touched the point with his index finger.

"Ouch!"

A drop of blood bloomed on his fingertip.

Serves me right, he scolded himself. *Going through Father's things.*

He sucked his finger, put the knife back in its resting place, and backed out of the armoire.

The city was quiet. No maglev trains zipping along the lines. No drones flying overhead. No kids on hover bikes. And no vendors selling their wares. There was only a grim silence that T'Challa found unsettling. People were afraid to leave their homes, he realized. The streets were never this empty.

T'Challa looked toward the western sky, shielding his eyes from the intense heat of the sun. Akema led them quietly, like a lone panther hunting for prey. T'Challa pulled a bottle of water from his pack and took a long drink. He looked back at Zeke and Sheila, trying their best to put on a positive face, but it was easy to sense their uncertainty and fear. Zeke kept wiping sweat from his brow and pausing to push his glasses up on his nose. Sheila wore a grim expression, ever vigilant. M'Baku, meanwhile, was silent.

The Necropolis was in an area on the outskirts of the capital. There was no entrance, nor any sign of welcome. You *knew* if you were supposed to be there. Or not.

T'Challa had only seen it once, from thirty thousand feet, when he was with his father in the Royal Talon Fighter as a child. That's when his father first told him it was the resting place of the dead.

It took hours to walk to the Necropolis, and by the time they arrived, he was drenched in sweat. T'Challa wiped his forehead with the back of his hand. He stood in front of the ancient structure and took it all in. Out here, there was no shade provided by tall buildings and structures, only a barren plain with one colossal maze at the center. The ground beneath his feet was made up of massive slabs of black stone.

"This looks . . . inviting," Zeke said.

"Tell me about it," M'Baku added. "I really don't think we should be here."

"You shouldn't," Akema said, her tone as sharp as a knife's edge. "But it is what the prince has demanded."

M'Baku grinned and opened his mouth, ready for a snarky comeback, but T'Challa shot him a quick warning glance and M'Baku held his tongue.

"Where?" T'Challa asked Akema. "Where do we find this . . . Zawavari?"

Akema peered into the distance. "It has been many years since I have walked in the City of the Dead," she murmured. "Zawavari could be anywhere. But when I accompanied the king here, we found him in a cave." She pointed a long finger into the distance. "That way."

T'Challa looked ahead. The Necropolis was an open-air structure built using horizontal and vertical stone beams, all with symbols and letters carved into them that he didn't understand. These beams were spread throughout, and one could walk through and under to go farther in. It reminded T'Challa a little of the monuments of Stonehenge, but where Stonehenge's slabs of rock were weathered and misshapen, the stone beams here looked smooth to the touch, as if they had been polished to a fine luster over the centuries.

T'Challa reached out and touched one of the giant beams. "Bast protect me."

As if in answer, a black cat slowly slunk between two beams, bristling tail held high.

"Uh," Zeke started. "That's a good omen. Right?"

T'Challa swallowed hard.

The air was cooler within the stone structures, as if a phantom breeze were at work. Dotted here and there, T'Challa saw what looked to be memorials, where people had laid flowers, fruit, and personal items to pay tribute to loved ones. He carefully stepped around them, wary of upsetting the dead.

"Look," Zeke said, pointing into the distance. "What's that big black shape way out there?"

T'Challa followed Zeke's finger. A giant shadow loomed farther away, a half mile from where they stood.

"A temple to Bast," Akema said. She dipped her head as if paying respect.

Up ahead, in front of T'Challa, several tall structures cast long, narrow shadows on the ground. As he drew closer, he saw what they truly were. These were the sarcophagi of Black Panthers of old. The lids were made in the image of men, with proud faces staring into the distance. They reminded T'Challa of mummified kings and queens he had once seen in Egypt with his father, when he had accompanied him on a visit. The outside world thought Wakanda was a poor nation, and often, other countries would invite the king for diplomatic talks. Little did they know of its real strength and history.

The sarcophagi were positioned upright and standing tall, as if the dead kings were forever keeping watch over the land they once protected. T'Challa ran his fingers along one of the upright coffins. It was cool to the touch. The head was that of a man, but the almond-shaped eyes were catlike. A headdress—a nemes, T'Challa thought it was called—framed the man's face and rested on his shoulders. Symbols were etched into the stone, but T'Challa could not read them. *What language is it? Shouldn't I know some of these things if I am to become the Black Panther?*

He suddenly remembered the strange symbols he had seen in the portal, where the Old Ones came through.

How did Tafari do it?

T'Challa wondered if Bashenga, the first Black Panther, was here somewhere. His own father would rest here as well one day, he realized. He turned away from the thought. He didn't want to think about that. Not here. Not now.

The others were quiet and walked carefully, whether out of respect or fear, T'Challa did not know. He continued onward and left the ominous sarcophagi and stone beams behind, his footfalls suddenly loud in his ears.

Ahead of them, a mound sloped up toward a large stand of trees. And in the center of that mound was an opening. A doorway.

"I guess that's it," Zeke said. "Where we—I mean you—go in."

"Prince T'Challa," Akema called as she turned and stood in front of him. "I do not know what danger may lie ahead of you. Zawavari is wise, but I have heard he sometimes speaks in riddles. He may also want something from you. Be careful, and we will wait for your return." Her green-eyed gaze rested on him for a long moment. "May Bast travel with you."

T'Challa swallowed the lump in his throat and looked to Zeke and Sheila, who both gave hesitant smiles.

"Be safe," Sheila said. "And come back to us."

"I will," T'Challa replied. "Promise."

He gave each of them a long, knowing look, and then made his way to the entrance.

As he drew closer, he noticed a soft red glow pulsating around the edges of the opening. To some, he imagined, it was an invitation; to others, perhaps, a warning.

He stepped through.

Darkness loomed ahead of him.

The walls were covered in moss, and the air smelled of freshly turned soil. A dim, red light pulsed within, just like the entrance. A ring of white rocks were to his left. He took a few steps and lowered his head to study the rocks. They looked ordinary, but some of them seemed as if they had been scorched by fire.

He walked for several more minutes, the drip of water pinging in his ears.

Should I call out?

Where could he be?

And how could someone live in here?

After a few more minutes, he turned around, one last look to see if he could still see daylight.

A man stood in front of him.

CHAPTER
EIGHTEEN

T'Challa's heart hammered in his temples. The man just stood there, studying him. His face was long and narrow, with slow-blinking, heavy-lidded eyes. An animal skin was draped around his shoulders, and the rest of his body was cloaked in darkness. Faint red spirals, like tribal tattoos, marked his cheeks, with one in the center of his forehead. Gold rings dangled from his ears.

So he's real, T'Challa thought. *I'm not imagining all of this.*

The cave suddenly felt stuffy, and he swallowed nervously. "I am Prince T'Challa," he said, in as strong a voice as he could muster, "son of T'Chaka. I seek your counsel, Zawavari."

There was a moment of silence, the only sound the dripping of water from the unseen roof. "I know who you are," Zawavari finally spoke, "and I know why you have come."

T'Challa shifted on his feet.

"You do?"

Zawavari took a few steps toward T'Challa. "Let me get a look at you. My old eyes are fading."

He shuffled toward T'Challa, leaning on a gnarled wooden staff for support.

T'Challa took small breaths, trying to appear calm as the old man studied him. He let Zawavari get very close, so close T'Challa could smell the scent of smoke and fire around him.

"Ah, yes, there it is," Zawavari said, drawing back. "I recognize you now. I see your father in those eyes. How is young T'Chaka?"

T'Challa almost smirked. *Young T'Chaka?*

How could this man not know what was happening outside of this cave?

"My father and mother are . . . missing. There was an attack. They were swept up in a whirlwind, along with many other leaders and elders."

"Is that so?" Zawavari asked.

T'Challa's patience was wearing thin. What, exactly, could this man do for him?

"I was sent here because I heard you could help. I need

a way to reach the ancestors and ask for guidance. I don't know where else to go."

Zawavari nodded and rubbed his whiskered chin. "There's the truth of it," he said.

He turned away from T'Challa and seemed to fade into a deeper shade of black in the cave. It was another opening.

T'Challa followed.

"Well?" he half shouted. "Can you help me?"

Zawavari didn't reply, only kept moving forward until T'Challa saw and smelled smoke. They entered a small room where a low fire burned. The walls here seemed to be carved from black rock.

"Sit," Zawavari said.

T'Challa looked down at the earthen floor. He sat before the fire and crossed his legs. With great effort, Zawavari lowered himself to the ground as well, and laid his staff across his knees.

"The troubles of Wakanda are no longer my concern," he said. "I dwell here, in what some would call a state of . . . transcendence. A higher plane, if you will."

The old man closed his eyes. T'Challa thought he was about to fall asleep, but he opened them and spoke again. "I once helped T'Chaka and Ramonda. They are good people. Of course I will help their son."

T'Challa sighed in relief but couldn't help but notice that Zawavari didn't use the honorifics *King* and *Queen* when speaking of his parents.

"There is, however, something you could do for me."

T'Challa tensed.

Zawavari's brown eyes grew wide.

Akema's words came back to him:

Zawavari is wise, but I have heard he sometimes speaks in riddles. He may also want something from you.

"If I can help you, I will," T'Challa said, and hoped he wasn't falling into a trap.

"Good," Zawavari said. "All is good."

The shaman reached into the folds of his clothing and pulled out a pouch. He unknotted the string and poured the contents into a small clay pot by the fire. It was a mortar and pestle, T'Challa realized. The scraping and grinding were loud in the cave as Zawavari did his work. It was a fine black dust, T'Challa saw, which seemed to sparkle with glittering white specks.

"To travel to the land of the ancestors, you must be clear of mind and spirit. Take this."

A gnarled hand reached into another pouch and handed T'Challa what looked like a root of some sort. T'Challa took it in his hands. It was soft to the touch and fibrous. "You want me to . . . eat this?" he asked, apprehensive. "What is it?"

"It is what will help you see," Zawavari replied.

T'Challa had no other choice. He had to trust him. He had come this far. If his parents had truly sought this man's advice at one point, he couldn't be all that dangerous. *I hope,* he thought.

The heat from the fire was strong, and beads of sweat dotted T'Challa's forehead. He fingered the root in his hand. "Here goes," he said.

Sensation flooded his mouth. It was like ginger root, clove, nutmeg, and chocolate, all in one. He swallowed with a gulp.

Zawavari studied him carefully.

"All gone?" he asked with a curious raised eyebrow.

T'Challa nodded.

"Good," the old shaman said.

"How will I get there?" T'Challa asked, the flavor of the root still on his tongue. "To the place of the ancestors?"

"You will ride on a curtain of fire," Zawavari said.

The shaman grinned, and T'Challa thought he had made a deadly mistake trusting him.

He tried to rise, but before he could stand up, the shaman cupped some of the powder in his hand and blew it at T'Challa's face.

CHAPTER
NINETEEN

T'Challa raised his hands to his face as a stream of flame shot toward him.

I've been burned!

He stumbled back, almost tripping.

He touched his face again. It was hot, but not from the heat of a flame. He was unharmed. He lowered his hands and exhaled.

He looked out at a dimly lit world.

There was neither sun nor moon, only an expansive lilac sky that gave the air a ghostly shimmer.

Where am I?

In the distance, trees swayed in an unfelt breeze. T'Challa

looked down to his feet. His mouth opened in shock. He was no longer wearing the clothes he had set out in. He was dressed in a white agbada, a garment similar to a robe. Stars seemed to wink within the fabric.

He began to walk, his breathing slowly returning to normal. He didn't know his destination. He just put one foot in front of the other and moved forward. The air was dry here but felt refreshing somehow. He took a deep breath, filling his lungs with the essence of this otherworldly place, trying to preserve the memory. His mind and body felt relaxed, as if he had just awakened from a long, fulfilling sleep.

Who will I see here? And what did Zawavari blow into my face?

The ground seemed to be a sea of black sand, sparkling under his feet.

Was that music in his ears?

It was a chorus of some sort. It was the most beautiful sound he had ever heard, and it lifted his heart in a way he had never felt before, which almost brought him to tears.

He pressed forward.

A baobab tree was up ahead, its bare trunk soaring to the sky, and at the top, a forest of leaves that seemed to brush the very heavens.

"Why are you here, Young Panther? It is not yet your time."

The voice was clear as a bell inside T'Challa's head, as if someone was standing right next to him. He spun around.

T'Challa froze.

A man stood before him.

A man who had his father's eyes.

"Grandson," King Azzuri the Wise said.

T'Challa studied the figure before him, his beloved grandfather. He didn't have any memories of him, but still, his heart swelled all the same. He wore a white agbada, the same clothing T'Challa had found himself in. His form felt substantial, but still slight, as if he could blow away on a strong wind.

"Surely it is not your time, T'Challa. Tell me, what brings you here?"

T'Challa couldn't believe it. Here he was, in the Ancestral Plane, talking to his grandfather. T'Challa's father had often regaled him with stories of the great king and how he fought with Captain America and the Howling Commandos. His grandfather had been an incredible fighter, and not one to show mercy.

T'Challa swallowed, coming back to the moment. "There is trouble in the kingdom, Grandfather. Father and Mother . . . they . . . they have been taken."

Azzuri's brow wrinkled. *"Taken? To where? By whom?"*

"A young man. His name is Tafari, and he is aided by another man called Silumko. They have used some sort of . . . sorcery to whisk the king and queen away to a place called the Nether-Realms." T'Challa released a breath.

"Walk with me, child," King Azzuri said.

And T'Challa did.

T'Challa looked at his feet as he walked, but he did not see any footsteps, nor did he see any of his grandfather's.

"T'Challa," Azzuri said. *"This plane of existence is not for the living. How have you come to this place?"*

T'Challa told his grandfather all about Zawavari and how he used magic to bring him here.

King Azzuri's expression grew grave.

"Zawavari always seeks something in return for his gifts. Be careful, T'Challa. He has power and sometimes uses it for his own gain."

"I will," T'Challa promised him, and wondered exactly how old Zawavari was.

"Now," King Azzuri asked, *"where did you learn of the Nether-Realms?"*

"In a book. In the Royal Library. It talked about the Old Ones. It said they were in Wakanda before Bast. But Tafari called them the Originators. He wants Wakanda to return to the past and worship them, to turn away from Bast."

The words came so fast from T'Challa's mouth, he had to pause for breath.

King Azzuri came to an immediate stop.

He turned to his grandson. *"T'Challa. Tell me everything you know."*

And that's what T'Challa did.

Afterward, as they sat against the great trunk of a baobab tree, King Azzuri sighed.

"What is it?" T'Challa asked. "Can you help me?"

King Azzuri shook his head. *"It is up to you, T'Challa. I cannot interfere in the world of the living, only give counsel."*

T'Challa's heart fell.

"So, what is your counsel, then? What should I do?"

King Azzuri laid a hand on his grandson's shoulder. His touch was as light as a feather. He was silent for a long moment. *"Only you can answer that. But there is one thing I can tell you that might help."*

A glimmer of hope sparked in T'Challa's eyes.

"The answer lies with Bast," King Azzuri said.

T'Challa waited for more, but his grandfather remained silent. A cool wind drifted across T'Challa's face.

"Is that it?" he asked, trying to keep a respectful tone. "That's all you can tell me?"

"I have told you all I can, T'Challa."

T'Challa shook his head in frustration. He was crestfallen. Had he come all this way for nothing more than a suggestion to pray?

I need more answers! T'Challa shouted in his head, but when he spoke, his voice was calm. "Grandfather?" he said, but the apparition of King Azzuri the Wise slowly faded, carried away by a breeze that T'Challa felt on his face and arms.

He was alone.

CHAPTER
TWENTY

T'Challa felt a pull, a tugging in his stomach as if someone had tied a rope around his waist.

"Grandfather!" he shouted.

Wind roared in his ears. The pull was greater now, and for a moment, he felt as if he was about to be sick, but suddenly found himself sitting beside the fire again, with Zawavari opposite him.

T'Challa took deep breaths and peered around the cave, trying to orient himself. "How? How . . . How did you do that? How did you . . . transport me to . . . to . . ."

Zawavari grinned, showing white teeth. "You, Young

Prince, remained here. It was your *spirit* that was traveling."

T'Challa raised his hand to feel his face and neck. A ringing buzzed in his ears.

"My spirit?"

"There are many ways to travel in this world, T'Challa, but not everyone knows the path of the mind."

T'Challa's head was still spinning. He had seen his grandfather. It had really happened. Or had it? He began to doubt himself. Maybe this shaman planted these thoughts in his head.

"Did you find the answers you seek?" Zawavari asked.

T'Challa paused. "I don't know. I mean, I'm not sure."

Zawavari laughed.

"I hope you did, Young Prince. Speaking of that, I have something I need from you."

T'Challa thought of standing up and running for the exit. Then again, if this man could send him to another plane of existence by blowing powder into his face, he could probably root him to the ground where he sat.

"What is it?" he asked.

Zawavari's brown eyes grew wide again. "When you take the throne, you must pay me another visit. We will have much to discuss, I am sure."

T'Challa squinted.

Is that it?

"Yes," Zawavari said, as if he had read T'Challa's mind.

"Now you must go, my friend. And remember, see me when the time comes. I will be here, as I always have, and always will be."

T'Challa stood up on unsteady legs. "Thank you," he said.

Zawavari bowed his head.

"Water," T'Challa begged as he walked into the waning light.

Akema was the first to see him, and she ran to him quickly.

"Are you hurt, my prince? Did he harm you?"

"No," T'Challa said, still in a daze.

Zeke rummaged in his bag and handed his friend a bottle. T'Challa drank greedily, rivulets of water dripping down his chin. Sheila studied him closely. T'Challa realized they were giving him a minute to recover, and none of them immediately bombarded him with questions.

"I saw my grandfather," he finally said.

Akema's eyes lit up. "King Azzuri?"

"Yes," T'Challa replied.

"Did he help?" M'Baku asked.

"What did he tell us to do?" Sheila added.

But T'Challa didn't answer right away. Instead, he asked, "How long was I gone?"

The sun was now setting, a thin line of orange in the western sky.

"A few hours," Sheila said.

T'Challa's sense of time was warped. His legs still felt unsteady. He took another small sip of water. "He said we had to figure it out . . . and that he couldn't interfere in the land of the living."

M'Baku punched his palm with a fist. "What good does that do? We need help . . . now!"

"I know," T'Challa said. He paused. "The only answer he had was to encourage us to trust in Bast."

"And that was it?" Sheila asked.

"Yup," T'Challa replied.

M'Baku turned in a circle and muttered at the sky. "Wait a minute," he said. "We came all this way and you took a journey to . . . wherever, and didn't get any answers?"

T'Challa didn't reply directly, and only stared at his friend for a moment. He felt as if he could collapse.

"We should get back," Akema said.

Sheila reached out for T'Challa's arm, and together, they all made their way back to the palace.

It took at least an hour for T'Challa's head to clear. As he walked, he noticed a radiance to everything around him. Eventually it faded, but his mind was still plagued with questions.

Back at the palace, they all gathered in T'Challa's residence. Everyone wore glum faces. Zeke lounged in a chair, half-asleep. Shuri paced and chewed a fingernail. M'Baku sat silent and brooding.

"So," Shuri started, her voice low. "What was it like? Seeing . . . grandfather?"

The memory was already beginning to fade from T'Challa's mind, but he tried to recall the feeling. "It was weird. Like a dream of sorts."

"I suppose it's a form of astral projection," Sheila said. "I never thought something like that really existed, scientifically speaking, I mean."

T'Challa had a vision of black sands and a lilac sky. The rich voice of his grandfather still felt close in his ears.

"It's real," he said. "Call it a dream, astral projection, or whatever. All I know is that I saw and talked to my grandfather, just like I'm talking to you right now."

Sheila leaned back against her chair. "Incredible."

"What was this shaman dude like?" Zeke asked.

"Strange," T'Challa said. "I couldn't figure him out. I wasn't really afraid of him, but he was . . . intense."

T'Challa closed his eyes. He needed answers but also rest. The murmur of voices sounded through the window. Raised voices. Sheila jumped from her chair. "T'Challa. You hear that?"

"What's going on?" T'Challa mumbled, the hope of a moment's rest dashed.

Shouts boomed from outside.

"What the—?" Shuri exclaimed.

Akema bolted around the corner and into the room. "Follow me! Now!"

They all hurried to the exit. Outside, T'Challa blinked.

A crowd of Wakandans huddled in the street, as if frozen by fear. It took a moment for T'Challa to focus on what he was seeing, but his eyes drifted toward a figure nearby, dressed all in white.

It was Tafari.

And he was not alone.

Two . . . *creatures* were with him.

One of them was a serpent.

And it was standing upright, balanced on its tail, scales gleaming in the waning light. Three arms protruded from each side of its torso.

T'Challa tasted bile in the back of his throat.

Today, we would call them demons. Supernatural creatures so old no one remembers their names.

Professor Silumko was there, too, standing beside another monstrosity pulled from the nightmares of children. It was spiderlike in appearance, an arachnoid standing on two feet, with a grotesque tangle of pincer-arms as weapons.

"Bast save us," Shuri whispered.

Tafari held out his arms and turned in a circle, as if welcoming guests to a performance.

"Behold!" he cried. "The new rulers of Wakanda!"

The snake creature hissed, and a forked tongue darted from its mouth.

"No," Zeke muttered, looking away. "No."

T'Challa tried to do the same, but he couldn't. He truly

couldn't believe what he was looking at. He tried to focus on Tafari and not let his gaze wander to the disturbing creatures, the Old Ones.

The Old Ones were unbearable to look upon and fearsome in their visage: horned, gilled, and feathered; beaked, clawed, and fork-tongued.

"T'Challa," Tafari called. "I have had an epiphany. Would you like to hear it?"

T'Challa didn't answer.

"You see," Tafari continued, speaking to T'Challa and the others as much as he was to those crouching in terror several feet away, "for a while, I was content to let your parents and the elders live, kept in a state of timeless eternity, unable to awaken. But now I have changed my mind, all because of your . . . stubbornness."

He paused, and T'Challa and his friends waited.

Should I tell Akema to attack? T'Challa wondered. *No, hear him out first.*

Tafari took his time, relishing the moment. "What I have decided to do, is to have them stand trial!"

"Trial!" Shuri scoffed. "For what? You're the one who will be judged!"

Tafari shook his head. "Ah, Shuri. So fierce for one so little."

Shuri muttered under her breath.

"And what is the charge?" T'Challa managed to shout.

Tafari smiled. "Traitors to the nation."

T'Challa gritted his teeth in anger. "My father is the ruling Black Panther and King of Wakanda! You, Tafari, are the traitor!"

The spider creature writhed, its arms waving in a grotesque display.

"Ignore me at your peril, T'Challa," Tafari warned him. "But they will be judged all the same. Your father and the so-called Black Panthers before him took this country from its original inhabitants by force. But the tide is turning. I have brought them forth again to claim what is rightfully theirs, and I will be the one who is rewarded!"

"You're out of your mind," T'Challa said.

"Perhaps," Tafari replied calmly. "But if you do not kneel before the Old Ones, your life will be forfeit, as will be the lives of your people. So I ask you, will you bend the knee? Choose wisely, T'Challa."

T'Challa looked at the Wakandans still motionless and rooted in place. He saw the terror and apprehension on their faces. Children were in the crowd as well, clutching their frightened parents. One man in particular stood out. He was old, as was the woman with him. They held on to each other tightly, as if afraid they would lose each other if they broke their embrace.

T'Challa struggled on what to do. He couldn't leave his people at the mercy of Tafari, but he had no choice. He was of the Panther Cult and of royal blood. And he would not yield.

He cast his gaze back to Tafari. "I will kneel to no man! Only Bast herself!"

At that moment, one of the creatures flew back and fell to the ground with a scream, its hideous hide pierced by a deadly spear.

T'Challa whipped his head around.

Cebisa, one of the Dora Milaje, had hit her target.

"No!" Tafari wailed.

The creatures around Tafari and Silumko shrieked in agony, as if they had all felt the sting of the Dora Milaje as well, but they did not advance.

"So be it!" Tafari shouted. "I have your answer."

T'Challa watched as Tafari placed his hands in his robe. Akema readied her spear, but T'Challa held up a cautious hand.

At first T'Challa thought Tafari was about to draw a weapon, and he crouched in a defensive position, but instead, Tafari held up two shiny objects. T'Challa was too far away to see what they were before Tafari raised them above his head and clacked them together.

There was a moment of eerie stillness, and then, as T'Challa and his friends watched, the air became charged and suddenly ripped apart where Tafari and his demonic allies stood. It was another portal, teeming with swirling blue energy. Dark, angry clouds passed overhead, and thunder rolled in the distance. The captive Wakandans fell to the ground. And then the most terrifying assault T'Challa had ever seen began. The helpless Wakandans began to drift toward the portal in a tangle of arms and legs. They screamed and clawed and grasped at the ground for purchase, but it was no use.

T'Challa ran forward.

"T'Challa, stop!" Shuri shouted, pulling him back.

T'Challa froze in place.

And watched as his fellow Wakandans vanished into the gaping hole of nothingness.

Tafari and the Old Ones were nowhere to be seen.

CHAPTER
TWENTY-ONE

Back inside, T'Challa tried to calm everyone's nerves. It didn't seem to be working.

"He's too powerful!" Shuri said.

"They just . . . disappeared!" M'Baku added, shock etched on his face.

"Big brother," Shuri started. "There was no way you could have stopped them. You would have been sucked up in that black hole, too!"

T'Challa didn't respond. He was raging inside. His people had just been abducted, and he wasn't able to stop it.

You're no prince. You'll never be as strong as your father.

Who will protect the nation now that the mighty Black Panther is gone?

T'Challa tried with all his might to remain calm, but his heart raced in his chest. Every lesson his father and mother had ever taught him flooded his brain, too quickly to make sense of.

Zeke, who had remained quiet, finally raised his head. T'Challa knew Zeke very well, and even after all the ordeals they had been through, he had never before seen his friend's face so stricken. "What were those things, T'Challa? How could anything be so . . ."

"Disgusting?" Sheila put in.

Zeke slowly shook his head. His eyes went glassy. "What can we do? It's . . . too much."

"He was holding something in his hands," T'Challa said, "before they disappeared."

"What could it be?" Sheila asked.

"Some kind of teleportation device," Shuri said.

T'Challa racked his brain for answers. It just didn't make any sense.

Another shout from around the corner made them all jump from their seats.

"They're back!" T'Challa hissed, bolting from his chair. The others followed his lead. Shuri snatched up a bust of a panther and held it cocked in her fist.

But it wasn't Tafari.

It was Akema, holding a dagger to a man's throat. His face was beyond frightened.

"My prince," he said, holding out his arms in surrender. "Please, tell her! I mean no harm!"

T'Challa looked at Akema, who shook her head in refusal, the blade still at the man's neck.

He couldn't do them harm, T'Challa saw, not with Akema's blade at his throat. He was empty-handed, and looked as if he was about to pass out.

"Release him," T'Challa said.

Akema pulled the blade away from his neck.

The man immediately gasped and clutched his throat, where, just a moment ago, he had felt the cold edge of a sharp, poisonous blade.

"Thank you, my prince," he moaned, almost falling over. "Thank you."

"Speak!" Akema commanded him.

Once the man seemed to regain some composure, he stood up fully. "Yes. I am sorry to disturb you, but there is something you must know."

T'Challa surveyed the man warily. He looked terrified, his eyes white with fear. "What is it?"

The man looked at Zeke and Sheila and turned back to T'Challa. "The . . . invaders. I saw where they came from."

Shuri set the panther bust back down.

T'Challa approached the man and stood close to him. "What is your name?"

"I am called Asefu, prince."

"Where did you see this, Asefu?"

"I was walking with my son. We were near the Valley of the Kings. There are woods there, Prince, a forest. I saw a light in the trees and . . . one of those things came out of it."

"Are you sure of this?" T'Challa pressed him.

"Absolutely, my prince. It was one of the ones who looked like . . . a serpent."

T'Challa turned and looked at his friends. "Take us there. Now!"

Night was falling as T'Challa and the others followed Asefu. Akema still watched him with a careful eye. T'Challa knew the way already. He had been there with Zeke and Sheila just a few days before.

"The Valley of the Kings," Zeke said. "That's where M'Baku said Bast's worshippers could turn into panthers, right?"

"Yes," T'Challa said. "Who knows if it's true, though."

"It's true," M'Baku said. "My father"—he paused and closed his eyes for a moment—"he said that his grandfather once saw a man do it. Right before his eyes."

"I believe it," Asefu said. He carried a knotted stick and peered around warily as he walked.

T'Challa learned that Asefu had two children at home, waiting for news of the king and queen. "I was there, my prince. At the Festival of the Ancestors." He paused and swallowed. "The snake men . . . What are they? Where do they come from?"

T'Challa didn't want to be evasive, but he also didn't want to frighten the man even more. "They are an enemy. That is all we know at the moment."

"But we will get your king back," Shuri said. "Our father and the queen will once again rule the nation."

"I believe it, Princess," Asefu said. "Glory to Bast, I believe it."

T'Challa smiled a little, hearing how this man trusted that peace would be restored. They were in the valley again, with magnificent white cliffs on either side. Above them, high up the mountain, was where the fabled city of Bastet supposedly once existed.

"It's just up here," Asefu said. "Around this corner."

Asefu led them to a dense thicket of moringa trees, their wide knotted trunks climbing skyward.

"Where?" Shuri demanded. "Where did you see it?"

Asefu stopped in his tracks and pointed, as if he wanted to go no farther. "Just there."

T'Challa followed Asefu's finger. Two trees stood next to each other, about six feet apart. The twisted branches of both trees met and formed an archway of sorts. T'Challa cautiously stepped forward.

"Wait," Akema said, holding up a hand. "I will go first."

T'Challa nodded and Akema took a few steps toward the archway. She walked slowly, eyes peering through the darkness. She reached the spot and looked left, then right, and turned back to T'Challa as if to say all was clear.

T'Challa and the others followed, until they were all standing in the archway. A chill swept through his body. "It's cold here."

"I feel it, too," Sheila said, rubbing her arms.

T'Challa peered into the space between the two trees. The air seemed to ripple, like a black curtain. "And you say this is where you saw it?" he called back to Asefu.

"Yes, Prince," Asefu replied. "There was a light, and the air seemed to part. That is when I saw the snake man. He stepped through, and then we ran."

T'Challa studied the ground at his feet, searching for any sign of the creature's presence. Akema did the same, even kneeling to pick up the soil and study it.

"What's this?" Zeke said, kneeling down.

They all gathered around to take a look. T'Challa's first thought was that it was a leaf, but it wasn't.

"Oh, god," Shuri said, leaning over Zeke's shoulder.

"What?" several voices asked at once.

Moonlight reflected what Zeke held in his hand.

"Those look like scales from a snake," Shuri told them.

Zeke actually shrieked as he dropped it and wiped his hands. "Gross."

T'Challa knelt and looked more closely. Growing up in Wakanda, he had been around animals all his life. "I think you're right, Shuri," he said. "That's definitely a snake scale."

"A large, *human*-shaped snake," Zeke added.

"Disgusting," M'Baku muttered.

T'Challa walked farther into the space between the two trees.

The first thing he felt was a resistance, as if there was some invisible force blocking his path. He reached out again and pushed with his hands, which were enveloped in cold air.

"What the—?" he said, reaching out and pressing again. "I can't get through!"

Akema was the next to try. She walked forward and reached out with long arms. She spread her fingers over the unseen wall, but gained no passage. She raised a foot and kicked, resulting in the same thing. "I feel bad energy here," she said. "Something is not right."

"Let me try," Shuri said, and reached out and tentatively pushed the air, only to be met by a solid wall. "Weird," she whispered, stepping back.

For a moment, they all just stood and stared.

"Definitely some kind of portal," Zeke finally said.

"So this is it, then?" Sheila said. "The door to the Nether-Realms?"

"The door to *somewhere*," T'Challa said.

"And we don't have a key," Zeke added.

M'Baku eyed the door as if it was a challenge. "We'll see about that," he boasted, and ran full speed at the space between the two trees.

"M'Baku, don't!" T'Challa shouted.

But it was too late.

M'Baku flew back five feet like he'd been shot from a cannon, landing on his backside. Gasps sounded all around. Akema almost chuckled. *Almost.*

"Are you okay?" Sheila asked, rushing to his side.

"Here," T'Challa said, offering a hand.

M'Baku grasped his friend's hand and pulled himself up. "Oof," he moaned, brushing leaves from his hair. "Shoulder hurts."

Shuri turned to Sheila. "Men," she said flatly.

Sheila shook her head in agreement.

"We have to find a way in," T'Challa said.

"It could be a trap, though," Zeke suggested.

"Look!" a voice cried out.

T'Challa spun around.

It was Asefu, pointing up toward the mountain.

T'Challa squinted into the darkness. Several figures could be seen standing on one of the outcroppings, a jagged ledge of stone. They were mere silhouettes, but T'Challa could distinctly see the shape of one of them. There was no mistaking that nightmarish form. A snake man. Several others joined him, some—surely Tafari's disciples—wearing white, as well as the hideous ones who resembled spiders.

"We better get back," T'Challa said. "We don't want to be seen."

"I say we fight," M'Baku said, rubbing his shoulder.

T'Challa turned to his friend. "With what, M'Baku?

Whose army? We don't have the firepower or a plan. To attack them would be a death sentence."

"My brother's right," Shuri said. "That is not the way."

T'Challa turned away from the view of the mountain. "We'll have to find another solution. That's all."

But in the back of his mind, a taunting voice asked, *How?*

CHAPTER
TWENTY-TWO

The group gathered at the Royal Library while T'Challa tried to figure out their next move. They were all exhausted. M'Baku was persistent on his plan to attack. "I say we round up every man, woman, and child that can wield a weapon and take the fight to Tafari!"

T'Challa was not convinced.

"The people are scared and frightened, M'Baku. The last thing I want to do is force them to fight. You saw those monsters. Our people would be slaughtered. They're not fighters."

M'Baku punched his palm with his fist. "What about

the Jabari Tribe? We can ask them for help. They are fierce warriors."

M'Baku had always admired and respected the mountain tribe, and T'Challa knew his friend had a special connection to them. M'Baku's uncle followed the path of the White Gorilla Cult, and T'Challa often wondered if his friend would join them when he came of age. But T'Challa also recalled what Silumko had said about Tafari, that his family was Jabari.

"No," T'Challa said. "They will not interfere. Plus, I don't want them knowing the palace is vulnerable. Who knows what they might try? You know they despise my father."

M'Baku nodded reluctantly.

Sheila and Zeke sat quietly, worry evident on their faces. Sheila appeared particularly disappointed, as she usually had a way of coming up with solutions, due to her skill in the sciences.

She sighed. "T'Challa. Maybe the answer is somewhere else."

T'Challa turned to his friend, as did everyone else.

Sheila clasped her hands together as she sat. Moonlight came in through the glass roof of the library and bathed her face.

"Your grandfather," she started, rising from her seat. "He said to turn to Bast for help." She paused. "Have you done that? Have you asked for her help in finding your parents?"

T'Challa was a little taken aback. He had never seen Sheila put any real faith in prayer. He knew her grandmother, Miss Rose, was religious, but he wasn't sure if her spirituality had worn off on her granddaughter.

"I always ask Bast for guidance," T'Challa said. "Every day."

"But have you really done it?" Sheila persisted. "I mean, actually asked for help."

T'Challa felt a tinge of embarrassment. "Well, I guess so."

Sheila nodded and began to pace. "Tell me exactly what he said again. Your grandfather."

T'Challa recalled the memory, although the actual experience of his visit to the otherworld was fading. "He said, 'The answer lies with Bast.'"

"Well, ask Bast, then," Sheila demanded. "I mean, *really* do it."

Shuri studied Sheila with a careful eye. "We know how to pray, Sheila. You don't get to tell followers of the Panther Cult how to—"

"It's okay," T'Challa interrupted. "Sheila's trying to help, and I need the reminder."

There was a moment of silence.

Have I really prayed? T'Challa asked himself. *Or have I just dismissed the idea?*

Shuri picked up on her brother's distress. "What?" she asked. "What is it?"

And that's when it struck him.

147

Could it be? he wondered. A puzzle, where words meant more than their initial meaning.

"Lies," he said.

Blank faces stared back at him.

"What lies?" Zeke asked.

"The answer lies with Bast," T'Challa whispered.

"Uh, okay," M'Baku said, tilting his head in concern. "We already know that."

"Don't you see?" T'Challa said, as if he was on the cusp of a great discovery. "Sheila made me think about it. *Really* think about it. The answer *lies* with Bast. *In* Bast. The answer is inside the Temple of Bast!"

CHAPTER
TWENTY-THREE

"Inside the temple?" Zeke ventured.

"What kind of answers could be in there?" M'Baku asked.

"I really don't know," T'Challa replied. "But I at least have to try."

"You mean *we* have to try," Shuri said. "I'll go with you, big brother. You might need help. You know I'm smarter than you."

"Me too," said M'Baku, standing up. "You need someone to watch your back, right?"

"Don't forget about us," Zeke put in. "If Sheila hadn't

mentioned that message from your grandfather in the first place, you might not have thought of it."

T'Challa already knew what he had to do. He just needed to tell them. And he was certain of his decision.

"I'll be going alone," he said.

"Nope," Shuri said, shaking her head in denial. "Nope. Nope. Nope."

"Good idea," M'Baku suggested. "Shuri should stay back and—"

"You're not going either," T'Challa said.

M'Baku looked as if he had been the last one chosen for a game.

"You don't mean to go alone, do you?" Sheila asked. "We're a team, T'Challa. Me, you, and Zeke. Remember?"

"Yeah," Zeke said.

"Not this time, guys," T'Challa told them. "Sorry. I don't know what I'm going to face in there, but something's telling me I have to do this alone."

Shuri crossed her arms, defiant. "All the more reason for us to go with you."

"It's a temple," T'Challa said firmly. "And it wouldn't be right for all of us to go traipsing through there, anyway."

"That's a good point," Zeke said.

Shuri still wasn't convinced.

"Sister," T'Challa said, placing a hand on her shoulder. "You need to stay here, near the palace. You are the Princess of Wakanda. If anything were to happen to you . . ."

The silence that descended hung in the air like a dead-weight.

"I will be here to protect her," Akema said. She had been listening to the whole debate, silent yet attentive.

T'Challa shot her a glance.

"We of the Panther Cult turn to Bast in times of great need," she said. "If now is not the time to seek her help, I don't know when is."

A weight lifted from T'Challa's shoulders. He had been sure that Akema would demand to travel with him, and he wasn't looking forward to an argument.

"It's settled, then," he said. "I'll leave in the morning. We all need rest after today."

His friends couldn't help but show their relief, knowing that they had time to sleep. T'Challa peered at each one of them, and lastly, at his sister. "I will be fine," he started. "I'll see you all in the morning."

As much as he desired it, a restful sleep didn't really come for T'Challa. Instead, he seemed to drift in and out of it, all the while accompanied by visions of Tafari and the Originators. He was glad when the first rays of the sun finally came through his window.

They all shared a quick meal before T'Challa's departure. None of them had been eating much at all, even Zeke, whose hunger was usually insatiable. Their dire circumstances had a way of killing an appetite.

"So, what do you think is in there, T'Challa?" Zeke asked.

"I don't know, Zeke, but I need to be ready for anything."

"In Egypt," Zeke went on, "some people think the Sphinx has hidden rooms and compartments."

"By *people* he means conspiracy theorists," Sheila put in.

"It's true!" Zeke said. "I saw it in a movie!"

"And what was this movie called?" Sheila shot back.

Zeke stared at his feet for a second and then looked back up. "Uh, it was called *Ancient . . . Conspiracies*."

M'Baku almost choked on his laughter.

Sheila shook her head in amusement.

"You should wear your suit," Shuri suggested, breaking the light mood. "Like you said, you don't know what you'll find in there."

Zeke's eyes lit up. Every time there was mention of T'Challa putting on the specially made panther suit, he got excited. One time he'd even asked T'Challa if he could wear it. The answer was no, of course. T'Challa's father had it specially made for him when he visited the States for the first time. It was insightful thinking, as T'Challa had to use it in some very tough situations.

T'Challa rubbed his chin. "No. I don't think it's right, Zeke. I'm not the Black Panther *yet*." He glanced at Akema, who actually granted him a small smile, the first time she had ever done so. "That would be my father. I don't want to show any disrespect in a place like that."

Zeke's face fell. "Wanted to see the suit," he mumbled.

"Maybe there'll be another chance," T'Challa said. "I think there just might be."

T'Challa said good-bye as he prepared to set out. "There's no way for us to communicate," he reminded them, "not with the network down."

"We'll be with you in spirit, big brother," Shuri said, and threw her arms around him.

T'Challa froze, his arms outstretched, until he finally returned the hug.

After they parted, T'Challa addressed Akema. "Alert Cebisa and Isipho and stay on guard. Tafari may be back, since we . . . killed one of his . . . monsters. He has our people hostage, and I don't want to do anything to threaten their lives even more. Keep watch and don't let my sister out of your sight."

Akema, ever ready to serve, drew a closed fist to her chest and dipped her head. "Travel safely, Prince. And we shall await your return."

"You better come back," Zeke said. He sniffed, which made Sheila sniff, too.

T'Challa felt his eyes sting but ignored it. Shuri crossed her arms over her chest and T'Challa followed suit, ending in a handshake they'd used since they were kids.

"And you're sure about this?" M'Baku asked, his voice unwavering.

"I am," T'Challa replied.

"Wait a minute," Zeke said. "Where is this temple, anyway?"

It was Akema who spoke up first. "There are monuments to Bast all over Wakanda."

But T'Challa knew of one in particular. It was the largest and most revered, and was said to be the oldest monument in the country. "I'll be going to the one near the Necropolis, where we were before."

A stillness descended, like a veil suddenly separated them.

"Come back safe," Sheila urged him. "Remember what your grandfather said: 'The answer lies with Bast.'"

T'Challa nodded, putting on his best face. "Thanks, Sheila. I wouldn't have thought of it if not for you."

"That's what friends are for," Sheila replied.

As T'Challa headed out, what his friends didn't hear was a whisper as he closed the door behind him: "Bast protect me."

CHAPTER
TWENTY-FOUR

The answer lies with Bast.

Grandfather would not lead me astray. He just wouldn't.

But was this really the answer? Was something hidden inside the Temple of Bast that could help them?

As T'Challa walked, he began to think about the invisible door in the forest. What would it take to get in? Magic? Brute force? And when and if he did, how could he rescue his parents and the people of Wakanda? All of these thoughts scrambled for attention and he tried to shut them out.

Focus on the mission at hand. One obstacle at a time.

With this mantra in his head, he quickened his pace.

The sun was high and bright and T'Challa felt its heat

on the back of his neck. It was a beautiful day, in stark contrast to his quest, a dark and possibly dangerous one.

He thought of his parents. Where, exactly, were they? Could they feel this same sun that bore down on him now? Were they cold and in pain? At least they were together, T'Challa tried to reassure himself, and they could draw strength from each other. All he could do was get to them as quickly as he could.

The bright sun was blocked by passing dark clouds as T'Challa approached the Necropolis. The stones and beams seemed to be an ominous warning: *Do not enter here.*

He walked slowly, not only out of fear but out of respect for the dead. He passed the upright sarcophagi of Black Panthers of the past. Jewels gleamed in their eyes, something he had not noticed before.

A wind stirred, and a slight rain began to fall. The dark cloud had now spread, and the sky suddenly became overcast. T'Challa hoped it wasn't an omen of things to come.

He saw the eyes first.

Blue eyes, glowing in the gray afternoon light.

The temple.

Bast.

T'Challa recalled those eyes. He had seen them before. *Run, Young Panther. Run.* They were words he had heard in another world, where Bast had once answered his call.

He tucked his head against the wind and rain and kept

moving forward, his gaze focused on the brilliance of those two blue orbs ahead of him.

The rain stung his face, and his legs ached. Even though he had a workout regimen that would tire most, he still felt the stress and fatigue. He needed a real rest, one that could refresh his mind and body. But there was nothing for it now but to move forward.

Like the Sphinx in Egypt, Bast lay crouched on her front feet, staring at any threat brave enough to enter. T'Challa stood in front of her mouth, which made him feel small and insignificant. It was an entrance, and the giant stone teeth were as tall as he was. *Are they sharp?* he wondered. *Now's no time to find out.*

Suddenly, Sheila's words came back to him:

Have you asked for her help in finding your parents?

T'Challa knelt. He wiped mist from his face.

"Mighty Bast," he started. "Protector. Mother. Goddess. I am T'Challa, son of T'Chaka. You have helped me before, and now I come to you again."

T'Challa swallowed, and his mind raced with what to say next.

"Your . . . messenger," he continued, "T'Chaka, son of King Azzuri the Wise, is in peril. His wife Ramonda, the queen, is also in danger. Our people . . . *your* people . . . are in deadly peril. I ask you, Bast, show me the way. Show me the path that may release them from this . . . evil."

He remained kneeling for a moment.

Was that enough? Should I say more?

He shook the thought away and stood up. "Ancestors protect me," he said, and stepped through a space between Bast's mighty teeth.

Chilly, moist air enveloped him, and he was reminded of Zawavari's cave. He waved his hand in front of his face: Darkness stared back at him.

T'Challa thought of his father and all the Black Panthers before him. He took another step. And another.

The answer lies with Bast.

Maybe Zeke was right, T'Challa suddenly thought. *I should've worn the suit. I'd at least be able to see better.*

No, it wouldn't be right, another voice countered. *You are not yet worthy of the mantle.*

T'Challa could *feel* the empty space around him. It was massive. He couldn't see the walls on either side of where he walked, but he could sense them. He walked slowly, putting one foot in front of the other, trusting that he wouldn't suddenly step into a hole and fall to his death.

"Who enters this solemn Temple of Bast?"

T'Challa froze.

His heart jumped in his chest.

It was a woman's voice, firm and strong, and it seemed to come from everywhere and nowhere at once.

He peered into the inky distance but saw nothing. He took a deep breath. "I am T'Challa. Son of T'Chaka, the Black Panther."

His voice seemed strangled in his throat, and a chill settled on his shoulders.

A light appeared in the distance.

And three figures came his way.

CHAPTER
TWENTY-FIVE

The figures seemed to be drifting toward T'Challa rather than walking, their robes sweeping the ground.

In one fluid motion, they came to a stop, five feet away. T'Challa took in the sight before him. Light seemed to radiate from their bodies, a shimmering, glowing aura. Two men, both with long dreadlocks and stern, sharp-angled faces, and a woman, taller than the men, with piercing white eyes that did not blink. A necklace of small bones encircled her neck. In her hand, she grasped an instrument T'Challa had seen before in a ceremonial tribute to Bast. The handle, which was about twelve inches long, rose up to an oval loop, and within that loop were several horizontal rods that held six flat bells, or cymbals. It was called a sistrum.

T'Challa was rooted to the spot. He blinked. It was hard to look at them, he realized; hard to meet their eyes, especially the woman's, whose gaze seemed to go right through him. The figures were so formidable and intimidating, T'Challa didn't know whether to bow or kneel. *Who are they?*

The woman raised her arm three times, ringing the sistrum. The bells echoed in T'Challa's ears, and he felt as if the sound entered his body and reverberated throughout his entire being.

"We are the Three," they said in unison. "Guardians of the Temple. Why have you come, T'Challa, son of T'Chaka?"

They just read my mind! T'Challa whisper-shouted inside his head.

He swallowed, and realized that his mouth was as dry as sand. "I come seeking answers. Wakanda is under attack. The king and queen have been taken." He licked his lips. "My grandfather, King Azzuri the Wise, said that the answer lies with Bast." He paused. "That is why I have come."

He hung his head, which seemed like the respectful thing to do in front of these mysterious beings. The silence seemed to last for an eternity.

"Only those who possess the blood of Bashenga may pass, T'Challa, son of T'Chaka," the woman said.

T'Challa wasn't sure what to say. He knew that his father came from a long line of Black Panthers, but did they all share Bashenga's bloodline? There was only one way to find out.

"I share the bloodline," he said, his voice confident.

The Three were silent, their expressions still impenetrable.

"Many have come and many have been turned away," the woman said. "What is it you seek?"

T'Challa shivered where he stood. He didn't know what he sought. *The answer* was all his grandfather had said.

"I am here to help my people," he said. "Whatever . . . answers you give would be . . . helpful."

A moment of silence passed until the woman shook the sistrum again, three times.

T'Challa's ears felt warm, like all his blood was rushing to his head.

"Come," she commanded. "Follow."

The Three turned in unison and T'Challa followed. It was still dark, but the light from the mysterious beings illuminated the ground where he walked. He looked at their garments. All wore loose-fitting clothing marked with symbols—the same symbols he had seen carved on the sarcophagi. He could feel his heartbeat thumping in time with his footsteps. *Where are they taking me?*

"To the place where truth is revealed," came the answer.

T'Challa closed his eyes for a brief moment. It was

unsettling to have someone inside your head. He wanted to empty his mind, but try as he might, it still raced.

The Three came to a stop in an area where a small fire burned. There was no wood or fuel, only flames that seemed to have a life of their own, ignited as if by magic, their flickering shadows dancing on the now visible walls, which appeared to be rock.

They turned around as one, and T'Challa saw that the woman now held a shining dagger in her free hand.

He gulped.

"This is the blade from the Spear of Bashenga, the first warrior blessed by almighty Bast. If you are who you claim to be, your blood will be true. Step forward, T'Challa, son of T'Chaka."

T'Challa had a decision to make. He could turn and run, flee from this strange place and try to resolve the conflict in another way. Or he could stay and accept their challenge, which was the braver but less sure choice.

He took a deep breath. Cold air filled his lungs.

And then he stepped forward.

CHAPTER
TWENTY-SIX

T'Challa didn't feel the cut on his open palm.

There was a sensation of cold, and then heat, but not pain. He closed his hand and felt the blood trickle down his wrist.

"Stand next to the fire."

T'Challa obeyed immediately.

One of the men held up his hands, palms open as if about to pray, and spoke, his voice as deep as the oceans. "We beseech you, Bast. Mother. Warrior. Sage. Blessed be the first warrior. May his blood prove his worth."

T'Challa swallowed. His palm now stung, but he still held it tight.

"Spill your blood upon the fire," the other man said with a voice just as solemn, "and the truth will be revealed."

This time, T'Challa didn't stop to start another internal conversation in his head. He slowly took a few tentative steps and opened his hand over the fire. Small drips of blood sizzled over the flame, turning the fire a spectrum of colors he couldn't even describe. He wondered what was supposed to happen, but the answer was soon given.

Ching! rang the sistrum.

As he stared into the fire, T'Challa saw, as if he were looking at a Kimoyo screen, images begin to dance in the flames.

He saw a man with a spear surrounded by panthers.

A woman veiled in black, her arms raised to the heavens.

A human figure with the head of a cat, walking with great strides in a forest of baobab trees. He saw faces, so many faces, flashing before his vision too quickly to comprehend.

A spray of green flame shot up from the fire, and the images winked out. It was an ordinary fire again, although one lit by unseen means.

T'Challa's breathing was loud in his ears.

Ching! rang the sistrum.

"The first test is true, T'Challa, son of T'Chaka," came the woman's voice again. "The blood of the first warrior runs through your veins."

T'Challa closed his eyes and sighed in relief. *Great,* he

thought. But what was the answer his grandfather spoke of? How could this help him in his quest?

The woman reached into her robes and withdrew a necklace. She stepped closer to T'Challa and put it around his neck. The necklace held a claw, gleaming white and curved to a sharp point.

"What is—"

"Come," she said, cutting him off. "This is only your first step."

Once again, T'Challa followed the ghostly figures.

T'Challa felt as if he had already walked the length of the monument, but the space seemed to expand the farther in they ventured. *What's next?* he wondered. *Not more blood, I hope.*

A sudden tingling started in his palm. He looked at his hand and blinked in disbelief. His palm was smooth and unblemished, as if a blade had not slid across it just moments ago. Was it his imagination? Had it really happened? The images still burned in his mind's eye, whatever they meant.

He fingered the claw around his neck. What was it? What did it do? Was this part of the answer his grandfather spoke of? *It's something,* T'Challa assured himself. *He did not lead me astray.*

Now they came to an area where the ground was like sparkling black sand, the same as T'Challa had seen on the Ancestral Plane. The fine grains winked in the darkness like stars fallen to Earth. And in that space was a hole. A grave. T'Challa shivered and closed his eyes in fear.

"Drink," the voices called, in unison this time.

T'Challa opened his eyes.

The woman stood before him, still unblinking, her eyes nothing but white orbs. The bones around her neck rattled. One of the men stepped closer and offered a wooden bowl, and T'Challa took it.

"Drink," came the command again.

T'Challa held the bowl with trembling hands.

He raised it to his lips.

The first drop to reach his tongue was warm and sweet, and it reminded T'Challa of the spice anise.

He stood there a moment, waiting for another command, but none came.

He opened his mouth to speak, but before he could say anything, his legs went out from under him.

He hit solid ground but did not feel any pain. He had the sense that he was being turned over on his back. He was surrounded by dirt. He felt it in his hair and on his bare arms, his mouth. He felt the black sand covering him, suffocating him.

I'm being buried! I can't breathe!

Ching! rang the sistrum.

And then darkness came.

CHAPTER
TWENTY-SEVEN

T'Challa found himself standing in a barren landscape. Dry earth spread out in front of him. He squinted from the bright sunlight and remembered that he had fallen into an open pit of black sand, yet here he was, walking and breathing. *Is it all in my mind?*

T'Challa almost panicked, but he suddenly remembered where he was and why. If these mysterious Three wanted to kill him, they would have done so already. He tried to ease his mind. *Relax*, he told himself. *Focus. I am T'Challa, son of T'Chaka.*

Slowly, he felt his heartbeat returning to a steady rhythm.

In the distance, spidery thin branches swayed in a wind he couldn't feel.

What is this place? What is here for me?

The ground beneath T'Challa's feet shook.

He reached out for balance, but there was nothing to give him support, and he almost fell to his knees.

When he raised his head, a figure was striding toward him.

T'Challa closed his fist. Was it a threat? Why would the Three send him here to die?

The figure drew closer, its form wavering in the bright sunlight.

Something was odd about the person's shape—if it was, indeed, a person. Whatever it was, it didn't have the head of a human, but a long, deadly-looking black beak. T'Challa felt the hair stand up on his neck.

Its head was that of an ibis, a water bird he had seen several times near lakes and streams, but its body was humanoid. It—he?—held a curved and hooked staff in his hand, and his eyes were black, as was his skin.

He faced T'Challa, silent. T'Challa didn't know what to do, so he gave a slight nod of his head, a sign of respect.

The being said something in a language T'Challa did not understand. But he never opened his beaklike mouth. T'Challa heard it *inside his head*.

Follow, he finally heard.

And T'Challa followed.

The man walked with a purposeful gait, and T'Challa was reminded of when he was a small boy, walking with his father, whose strides were so long T'Challa had to run to keep up. He didn't run now—that would have been strange in a place like this.

It was quiet. Deathly quiet. And hot. A hazy sun drifted between the streaky clouds. T'Challa had a sudden craving for water. His throat was parched.

Where is he taking me?

The man was big, with broad shoulders and legs like tree trunks. He wore sandals, a curved golden collar around his neck wide enough to span from shoulder to shoulder, and blue cuffs around his wrists and biceps.

T'Challa had a sudden memory of the Orishas. This was Thoth! He should have known immediately, but his senses had been overwhelmed.

Am I in the company of the gods?

Finally, they came to a swift-running stream. Thoth stopped and turned around. T'Challa shuddered, standing before such a powerful deity. He heard a voice inside his head that said:

Behold, I am the God-Bird; Ibis the Invincible; the Lord of Divine Words. Drink from the river, T'Challa, son of T'Chaka. Drink, and be purified, if your soul is true. But beware, for those who are not true, the water will turn to ash in your mouth.

The echo of Thoth's words seemed to ring in the air around T'Challa.

Thoth pointed his hooked staff toward the river.

That's not so hard, T'Challa thought. *It's just water.*

But Thoth's ominous warning stuck in the back of his brain.

. . . turn to ash in your mouth.

T'Challa knelt by the river's edge. He felt cool air on the back of his neck. The air was rich with scent, and T'Challa wasn't sure if it came from Thoth or the river itself. It was the odor of an ancient world, one of myrrh and woodsmoke; pomegranate and lavender; moth-riddled papyrus, and the pungent smell of flowering lilies.

T'Challa cupped his hands in the stream. It was ice-cold. He could taste it before it even reached his lips.

He brought his cupped hands up to his mouth.

He drank.

A searing pain ripped through his stomach.

He fell back, stunned.

"No!" he croaked. "What is happening?"

He coughed and spat water from his lungs.

Thoth stood over him, as if waiting, his shadow completely covering T'Challa's body.

T'Challa's coughing faded. He took deep gulps of air and looked up at the great figure towering over him.

To drink from the River of Death and live is an omen of a pure soul. Rise, T'Challa, son of T'Chaka.

Thoth extended a long arm, which, to T'Challa's swirling head, seemed larger than life. He saw a sparkling ring on one finger. . . .

Ching! rang the sistrum.

T'Challa gasped for breath.

He bolted upright.

He was back in the belly of Bast again. The Three stood silently, as if they had never moved. *How long have I been gone? Where was I?*

He brushed black sand from his face and waited for his breath to steady. Something glinted at the edge of his vision. A ring encircled the index finger of his left hand. A decorative eye, lustrous as a brushstroke, with a green gem at its center.

Thoth's ring. How?

"There is one more trial, T'Challa, son of T'Chaka," the voices rang out. "The time of the flame has come."

CHAPTER
TWENTY-EIGHT

T'Challa had no perception of time. Night or day, noon or midnight. He didn't remember when he'd entered the Temple of Bast. But he knew he had. He now felt neither hunger nor thirst, only fatigue, as if he could fall where he stood and sleep for the rest of his days.

But the Three had other plans.

Once again, T'Challa followed them.

He had a ring and a claw necklace. Surely these things were needed to help rescue his parents, but how?

T'Challa followed the—what were they? Captors, guides, spirits? He wasn't sure. So far, they had not harmed him, but their grave looks and demeanor still left him shaken.

The room they led him to was a long hall, where, at the very end, a chair sat. It was more like a throne, T'Challa realized. The back was studded with gemstones. The wall behind it showed carvings of a great battle. T'Challa could almost hear the hoofbeats of the charging riders and the horns being blown. He stepped closer, trying to make out the details of the stone tapestry. "Where was this battle?" he asked, turning around.

The Three had disappeared.

He turned back to the tapestry.

And saw a man with a head of flame sitting on the throne.

He held a great flaming staff in one hand. The heat reached where T'Challa stood, and he felt as if his eyebrows were singed. He could barely focus on the man in front of him because the fire from his body was so bright.

This can't be. How is this possible?

A dark space within the flame, which T'Challa took to be a mouth, opened, and the man stood up.

"Come, T'Challa, son of T'Chaka. Come and stand before my flame."

T'Challa wanted to flee this time. This was too much. He was frightened, and his legs trembled at the sight of the fire-headed figure.

But something drove him forward.

Perhaps it was the strength that his mother and father had instilled in him.

Perhaps it was his friends back home, waiting and trusting in his return.

Or perhaps it was the will he had found inside himself to accomplish this task, once and for all, and return to the land of the living.

He took a step forward.

And another.

The heat was almost unbearable.

He squinted as he drew closer, eyes almost completely shut. There was no smoke, only a red heat brighter than the sun.

T'Challa stood before the man with the head of flame. The strange figure was adorned in battle armor from the waist down. T'Challa couldn't see what else he wore because to look into that face would be certain death, he assumed.

The fiery mouth opened again, and the heat was like that of a furnace stoked with coal.

I am Kokou, the Ever-Burning, God of War. Take the scepter from my hand and I will release you from this place. If your soul is true, you will fear no harm.

T'Challa wiped his face with the back of his hand. His breathing was rapid and his eyes watered.

Kokou, another of the Orishas. How is this happening?

Just grab the staff—the scepter. I've been okay so far. This is just another test. That's all it is. Another test. Another test . . . another . . .

T'Challa squeezed his eyes shut and reached out for the staff.

He waited for the fire to consume him—to turn his hand to ash, ignite his body— but the flame was cool. He opened his eyes the exact moment the scepter's flame was extinguished.

Voices sounded behind T'Challa.

He spun around.

It was the Three again.

"You have passed the trials, T'Challa," the woman said. "Come. Stand before us."

This time, T'Challa came forward without hesitation.

"With the Claw of Bast, you will pierce the veil between worlds," one of the men said.

"With the Eye of Bast, you will see into the beyond," said the other.

"With the Scepter of Bast, your enemies will flee before you," said the woman with white eyes.

T'Challa stared at the otherworldly beings. "Who . . . who are you?"

"We are the Guardians of the Temple, Keepers of the Claw of Bast, which is what you now hold. Three pieces that came from one, blessed by almighty Bast."

T'Challa reached up and felt the claw around his neck.

The ring sparkled in his peripheral vision. And the staff he held in his hand was strong.

"Go now," the woman said. "Wakanda is calling you, Young Panther. Throw down your enemies, for they have brought evil upon the land. They are the Anansi and the Simbi, the spider and the snake, our old tormenters. Seal them in the Nether-Realms and lock the gate. The time will come only once."

And then, in one strong voice that seemed to shake the very walls of Bast's temple, they cried out, *"FLEE!"*

CHAPTER
TWENTY-NINE

T'Challa shaded his eyes with the edge of his hand. Spots danced in his vision.

How long was I gone?

It was still daylight, and the dark clouds had passed. But he didn't remember walking out of the temple. He had just found himself outside it, as if he had been magically transported.

It took a moment for him to steady himself, and he felt unsure of his steps. But, with the scepter in one hand, he made his way forward. The ring on his finger and the claw around his neck sparkled in the bright sunlight. If anyone saw him they would think that he was a shaman or conjurer.

The Claw of Bast. The Eye of Bast. The Scepter of Bast. These three totems would be used to reach the Nether-Realms. All he had to do was find out how.

T'Challa mused on what he had just gone through. He had met the Orishas. The *gods*. Thoth. Kokou. But what of the others? Were they also in that place but hidden from his view? He would probably never know. He passed a few people who didn't even give him a second glance. He looked down at his clothing and realized that he was covered in dirt. A burn mark was on his shirt. Not quite the Prince of Wakanda at the moment.

Sweat streaked his forehead as he got closer to home. He hoped his friends and sister were safe. They were probably very worried by now. By the time he reached the palace, his throat was parched and his tongue felt swollen.

"I'm back," he said, and then he collapsed.

T'Challa's friends gathered by his side. He was lying down, resting, and just coming to the realization that he had experienced something that few ever would. He had to tell the story twice for them all to fully understand. Akema's eyes were wide with wonder as he spoke. Much to T'Challa's shock, he'd been gone longer than he had thought.

"What do you mean?" he asked. "I came back today, the same day I left."

Sheila and Zeke traded glances. "That was yesterday, T'Challa," Sheila said. "You were gone for a whole day.

Akema was climbing the walls, about to go in search of you before you returned."

Akema nodded in agreement. T'Challa's head spun. *The whole day?* He couldn't believe it.

"Well," Zeke said, "you're back now, and safe. That's all that matters."

T'Challa released a ragged breath. The ring stayed on his finger and the claw around his neck. The scepter was by his bedside. He wasn't even sure if others were allowed to touch them, so they stayed clear.

M'Baku eyed the objects warily. "So, what do they do?" he asked.

"Do they have special powers?" Zeke asked, excited.

"They do," T'Challa replied. "But I'm not exactly sure how to use them."

"I'm more interested in the beings that you saw," Shuri said. "Do you really think they were the Orishas?"

An image of flame and smoke flashed in T'Challa's head. He looked at his palm, still smooth and unblemished. *I am the Ever-Burning*, one had said. *Behold, I am the God-Bird; Ibis the Invincible*, another had told him.

"They were," he said. "I know they were. Who else could they have been?"

No one had an answer.

T'Challa closed his eyes. He hadn't realized how truly tired he was. "The Three, they . . . said something else, too."

All eyes fell on him.

"They said that these Originators are called the Anansi and the Simbi—the spider and the snake—and that they were their tormentors from the past. They said to seal them in the Nether-Realms and lock the gate."

There was a moment of silence.

"Lock the gate," Sheila whispered.

"I don't have any idea how," T'Challa confessed.

"Maybe one of the . . . things they gave you," Zeke ventured. "Maybe they can be used to do that."

"I hope so," T'Challa said. "Bast willing, I hope so."

He shifted his weight on the bed. Sleep tempted him.

But he couldn't.

Not now.

He stood up.

"Prince," Akema started, her voice suddenly tense. "What are you doing? Where are you going?"

"I'm going to rescue our people."

"Not without me you aren't," Akema said, and then, cautiously: "My prince."

"You need to rest first, T'Challa," Shuri said. "A cloudy mind brings no rain, remember?"

"Good one," M'Baku put in.

T'Challa looked at his friends. Their faces were somber. He picked up the scepter and headed for the door. "Not this time," he said. "It's time to put on the suit."

CHAPTER
THIRTY

T'Challa lifted the panther suit from a velvet-lined box. He ran his fingers along the fabric. It was made of a Vibranium mesh that, if inspected closely, resembled a honeycomb pattern. He had only worn it twice before. Once in Chicago and another time in Alabama. Now he would use it in Wakanda.

Whatever awaited him in the Nether-Realms would be better faced with the protection of the suit. He slipped it on and looked at himself in the mirror. Memories came flashing back—a battle with a demon in an underground lair; fighting the Reverend Doctor Achebe in an abandoned mine in Alabama. The panther suit felt good on him, as if it had been waiting for him to wear it again. It was like diving into ribbons of black silk, soft, yet strong.

The suit was a marvel of Wakandan technology. It absorbed kinetic energy, storing the force of a blow to be redirected at an opponent. T'Challa stood in front of the mirror.

"I'm coming for you, Tafari."

Zeke smiled when he saw his friend enter the room.

"That's what I'm talking about right there!" he half shouted, barely able to contain his excitement.

Akema looked at Zeke with a stone-faced expression.

Zeke wilted. "Just sayin'," he whispered.

T'Challa gave a weak smile and shook his head.

Akema studied T'Challa with a careful eye. "It suits you, my prince," she said. "Worn like a king in waiting."

T'Challa exhaled.

Shuri and the others were prepared as well. Vibranium Gauntlets were locked on both of Shuri's hands. If one were to look at them head-on—as an enemy would—one would see two snarling panthers, eyes flaring red before they released a blast of sonic energy.

"What do you think, big brother?" she asked. "Wait till those snake men get a blast of these!"

"Where'd you get those?" T'Challa asked, surprised.

"I gave them to her," Akema said. "If this is truly war, we must be prepared."

"Yeah," Shuri said. "I know how they work."

A bolt of blue lightning blasted out of one of the gauntlets and left a smoking hole in the wall.

"Not sure that's a good idea," Zeke muttered.

M'Baku fell over laughing.

T'Challa looked at the smoking, grapefruit-sized hole. "Right," he said.

Akema rushed to Shuri and showed her the buttons for the proper firing technique. "Easy," she said. "The ignite button is touch-sensitive. Never point unless you are prepared to use it."

T'Challa was torn. He knew the gauntlets were a powerful weapon, but he wasn't sure if his little sister should be in the thick of battle if it came to that. He shot her a skeptical glance.

"What?" she said, defensive. "Don't tell me you don't want me to fight! Because, with Bast as my witness, I am!"

"Can't argue with that," Zeke said, admiring the gauntlets.

"We need every defense we can muster," M'Baku put in. He was holding a spear with a shining tip. "I picked this up when you were gone. It belongs to my mother. She calls it Assegai. You know how fierce she is, T'Challa."

"She is a great fighter," Akema said. "We Dora Milaje know her skills."

M'Baku beamed.

T'Challa couldn't help but smile.

"What about us?" Zeke asked. "What will we use?"

"Yeah," Sheila added. "There has to be something we can do to help."

"I thought of that, too," Shuri said. She took off the gauntlets—carefully—and dug around in a leather bag. T'Challa looked on curiously. *What is she up to now?*

Shuri pulled out a cloth pouch. She untied the drawstring and reached inside. T'Challa watched as she retrieved several small black oval discs.

T'Challa's eyes lit up. "Those are Father's EMP beads!"

"They used to be," Shuri said, grinning. "I deactivated the electromagnetic pulse mechanism, and now they're little bombs!"

T'Challa and the rest of the room froze.

T'Challa took a step forward. "Shuri . . ."

"Ah, don't worry," Shuri said. "They have to strike something for the charge to detonate."

"Cool," Zeke whispered, a mischievous gleam in his eye.

"Just," T'Challa started, "be very, very careful, guys."

Shuri handed Zeke and Sheila the beads. "Don't worry about them being in your pocket. They should be fine."

T'Challa closed his eyes in resignation.

"So," Sheila said, studying one of the small beads. "How, exactly, did you hack these?"

T'Challa drank several glasses of water before they departed. He was tired beyond belief, but his fellow Wakandans needed their help. The time to act was now, fatigued or not. Everyone gathered around him.

"Listen," he said. "First we head to that invisible door in the woods to see if we can find a way in."

As soon as he spoke the words, he realized just how absurd they sounded. Could they really do it? How did they even know if that invisible door was really an entrance? And if it was, how could they be expected to retrieve his parents and the others? If it was secure enough to imprison the Originators for generations, how could T'Challa, Akema and a few kids get his parents out of there? He looked at the ring on his finger and touched the Claw of Bast necklace. *With these, I hope. With these.*

T'Challa studied his sister and friends. Shuri was armed with her gauntlets, and M'Baku had his mother's spear. Akema had her own trusty spear, too, along with a Vibranium shield and daggers in every fold of her uniform. She had given the order to Cebisa and Isipho to stay alert and keep an eye on the palace. They had even recruited several loyal adults and armed them with weapons, blocking the entrance and stationed at important points around the city. T'Challa was glad to hear it. Who knew where Tafari would pop up next? He had already seen how he could appear and vanish in an instant. How did he do it?

Zeke and Sheila tried to put on brave faces, but T'Challa could see they were just as nervous as he was.

Akema caught T'Challa's eye and held it.

"Wakanda forever!" she cried out, and clashed her spear against her shield.

And they all repeated the call.

CHAPTER
THIRTY-ONE

The afternoon sky was threatening rain, and angry clouds loomed to the east as T'Challa led the way to the invisible door. Everyone was quiet, knowing what lay ahead of them. T'Challa took in the streets as they walked. He felt as if the capital was falling into disrepair. Maglev trains were stalled on the tracks, motionless. Clocks were stopped. Vibranium was a resource that was not only used as defense for the nation, but one that also powered everyday technology like clocks, heating ducts, and air-conditioning. How had Tafari knocked out the system?

T'Challa couldn't think on that now. He only had room

in his mind for one problem at a time, and rescuing his parents was the most important one.

T'Challa wore a lightweight cloak so as to not draw attention to himself in the panther suit, although the streets were mostly empty. Graffiti was not something one would normally see in Wakanda, but T'Challa and the others had noticed several spray-painted buildings, their messages each conveying a different concern:

GLORY TO BAST, WE WILL SURVIVE!

WHERE IS THE BLACK PANTHER?

FROM THE ASHES WE WILL RISE!

And some, alarmingly, were in support of Tafari and his crusade:

VIBRANIUM IS A CURSE!

IT IS TIME FOR A NEW REVOLUTION!

T'Challa passed the proclamations without comment.

He should have done more, he thought. Should have addressed the nation more than once. They needed a leader, and so far, he had failed them.

WHO WILL PROTECT THE NATION NOW THAT

THE MIGHTY BLACK PANTHER IS GONE?

I will make it up to you, T'Challa promised. *I will see our nation strong once again.*

"Tell me more," Sheila said, snapping T'Challa out of his thoughts, "about what you went through."

T'Challa felt as if the memory of it was already fading, but he searched within his mind for what else he could recall. "It was the strangest thing I've ever experienced, Sheila. The Three—I never learned who they were. They just said that they were the Guardians of the Temple and Keepers of the Claw of Bast, three pieces that came from one."

T'Challa paused and tried to recall more. "They seemed . . . ancient, somehow, like they had been in the world for generations. When they weren't speaking, I heard them inside my head."

He fell silent.

"It's good that you went," Sheila said. "I know it was hard, and that you took a chance on going there, but you came back with answers."

"And some cool stuff," put in Zeke, who had crept up beside them.

T'Challa managed a smile.

"There's something I've been meaning to ask," Zeke started, "but I didn't want to throw too much at you as soon as you got back."

"Okay," T'Challa said. "What is it?"

"That ring. The Eye of Bast, you called it. Do you think it has special powers? Like, um, turning you into a panther?"

T'Challa almost laughed. He wasn't sure if it was a myth

or not, but after seeing the Three and meeting the Orishas, he figured anything was possible.

"I'm not sure, Zeke. I guess we'll just have to see."

Zeke frowned. "Because, you know, if you don't want to fiddle around with it, I could—"

"I don't think so, Zeke," T'Challa said, cutting him off.

Sheila laughed and shook her head in disbelief.

"What?" Zeke complained, throwing his hands up in the air.

Once more into the valley they went. The ridged, jagged peaks and outcroppings of stone loomed above them. T'Challa saw no silhouettes of snake men this time.

"Be on your guard," Akema warned the group. "We saw them at the mountaintop last time. They might be able to see us from this distance."

Heeding Akema's warning, they moved farther up in the woods along a ridge of trees blocking the view from the mountain.

"Not too far now," Shuri said.

T'Challa heaved a breath and made his way forward.

He remembered the man, Asefu, who had shown him the mysterious door. He said he had two children at home, hoping for the return of the king. *I will not let you down, brother Asefu.*

Dread crept over T'Challa as he saw the two moringa

trees ahead of him. The archway of branches was still there, waiting. . . .

Akema readied her spear.

Shuri clicked a switch on her gauntlets, and they revved up with a whirring sound.

M'Baku crouched with his mother's spear, his gaze focused and alert.

Sheila and Zeke, T'Challa's best friends—friends who had stuck by his side every time—clutched the small bags of detonators, trying their best to appear brave, despite their shaking hands.

And T'Challa himself, the young prince of Wakanda, stood tall—the Claw, Eye, and Scepter of Bast at the ready.

"Let's do this," he said.

CHAPTER THIRTY-TWO

T'Challa tried to recall what the Three had told him. It was the one thing he truly remembered with clarity:

With the Claw of Bast, you will pierce the veil between worlds. With the Eye of Bast, you will see into the beyond. With the Scepter of Bast, your enemies will flee before you.

He fingered the claw around his neck. "'Pierce the veil between worlds,'" he said. "That has to be it!"

"What?" Zeke and Sheila asked at the same time.

"This claw," T'Challa said. "I think it'll open the door."

He gave one last look at his friends, lastly resting on Akema. "I'm not sure what's going to happen, but I don't think the Three would lead me astray. Everyone be ready."

He removed the chain from around his neck and gripped the claw between his fingers, sharp point facing out. "Here goes," he said, as he reached out to the space between the trees.

A great wind stirred the uppermost branches above them. Everyone tensed, peering around warily.

"Look!" Zeke shouted, pointing up to the mountain.

Along the edge of the outcropping, dozens of Simbi and Anansi were gathered. A roll of thunder cracked and then several things happened at once.

A loud clack, like two objects slamming into each other, sounded in T'Challa's ears, accompanied by a flash of white on the mountain. The next thing T'Challa knew, Tafari and several of the Originators were only a few steps away, as if they had materialized out of thin air.

"How in the world . . . ?" T'Challa started.

But there was no time to stop and think on it. "Stay alert," he whispered.

One of the snake men hissed as he had before, forked tongue flicking.

Tafari halted only steps away from T'Challa and glanced at Zeke, Sheila, and the others with disdain. "I gave you a chance, T'Challa, but you spilled the blood of one of the ancients. That cannot go unpunished." He turned his gaze to Akema, who gripped her spear with both hands. "You will pay for what you have done."

Akema ignored the threat and kept her spear aimed.

Tafari turned back to T'Challa. "I suppose you will not be honoring my command to bow before the Originators?"

"We bow to no man, only Bast," Shuri said, her gauntlets pulsing red.

"That is too bad," Tafari declared in mock sincerity. He turned to his hideous companions. "Take them."

Shuri fired her gauntlets, knocking two of the Originators back several feet in a concussive blast.

T'Challa threw the necklace back around his neck, and gripped the scepter with a sweating fist. *I don't know what power you hold, but don't fail me now!*

He swung the scepter in a wide arc, striking one of the Anansi, sending it hurtling back, pincer arms clawing the air.

Zeke and Sheila had retreated farther into the woods. Their first reaction was to run, but Sheila grasped Zeke by the arm. "Wait!" she whisper-shouted as they took cover.

"One," Sheila began, taking one of the missiles from her bag.

"Two," Zeke said, following her lead.

"Three!" they both shouted, and flung the detonators.

The force of the explosion uprooted a tree, scattering branches and leaves to the ground. M'Baku was hit by one of the falling limbs, but it did not deter him from using his spear to fend off one of the Simbi slithering toward him.

T'Challa flinched from the explosion but soon saw that his companions were not injured. With his heart in his throat, he planted his feet wide apart, and, gripping the scepter with both hands, raised it up and slammed it into the earth.

The ground split asunder with a terrible crack.

Several of the hideous creatures fell into the gaping hole.

T'Challa froze for a moment in disbelief.

With the Scepter of Bast, your enemies will flee before you.

"The portal!" Shuri shouted. "Now, T'Challa!"

Zeke and Sheila scurried from the safety of the dense woods and joined T'Challa and the others. Akema and M'Baku used their spears with deadly accuracy, keeping the monsters away from the future King of Wakanda.

But Tafari wasn't done yet.

He lunged at T'Challa, a dagger held high in his hand.

M'Baku jumped in front of T'Challa, holding his spear like a staff and blocking the blow.

Tafari fell back, white robes twisting around him.

"Now, T'Challa!" M'Baku cried out.

T'Challa, heart racing, turned and faced the space between the two trees. He grasped the claw on its chain and ran it down the invisible door in a slicing motion. Fiery sparks immediately danced in the space, blue energy swirling and flashing, revealing a doorway.

"It worked!" Zeke cried out.

Tafari scrambled up, and in doing so, something fell from his robes. T'Challa quickly recalled he had seen Tafari fiddling in his pockets before, when he threatened them at the Royal Library.

Tafari looked to the ground, fear suddenly evident on his face. He reached down.

But Sheila beat him to it.

And scooped up two gleaming objects.

"No!" Tafari cried out, reaching with long arms toward the invisible crack in the door.

But it was too late.

T'Challa and his companions slipped between the trees, with Tafari's bellowing screams echoing behind them.

CHAPTER
THIRTY-THREE

T'Challa peered around quickly, breath still coming fast. "Everyone okay?" he asked.

To his relief, they were all accounted for, but considerably disoriented. They all studied themselves for a moment, as if to make sure they hadn't left an arm or leg behind.

They seemed to be outdoors, judging by the breeze on T'Challa's face. There were no trees or structures of any kind, just a vast emptiness. The ground beneath their feet was black and rocky, almost volcanic, T'Challa thought. The only familiar sight was a blanket of stars that glittered overhead.

"Is this it?" Zeke asked. "The Nether-Realms?"

Shuri still had her gauntlets on her hands, and looked around as if snake men could arrive at any moment. Akema peered at their new environment with wary eyes.

T'Challa stitched their last few moments back together. He had sliced his way in at the last minute with the Claw of Bast and slipped through. Tafari was yelling, and Sheila had picked up two objects that had spilled from his robes.

"I have no idea what these are," Sheila's voice piped up through the dark. Everyone gathered around. Cupped in each of her hands were two small decoratively painted metal frogs, with red gemstones for eyes.

"What in the name of Bast are those?" Akema asked.

"Frogs," Zeke said flatly.

"They look like they're made of brass," Shuri put in. "Why would Tafari have these?"

"I think they're some kind of teleportation device," Sheila said, studying the objects. "Back in Wakanda, Tafari and his creatures were at the top of the mountain, and then they were standing in front of us in the blink of an eye."

T'Challa thought back to the moment when he had seen Tafari raise his hands above his head before he and his monsters had all vanished, along with the unfortunate prisoners. "I think Shuri's right," he said. "If he can use these to travel through time and space, maybe we can do the same."

"And get our people out of here," M'Baku added.

"Exactly," T'Challa said. "Now, everyone, follow me. And stay close."

They all fell in line behind T'Challa, every one of them on full alert. Akema took up the rear. It was dark, but there was just enough light to see by, although T'Challa couldn't find its source. It seemed natural, like moonlight but without a moon. The only sound was the soft weight of their feet as they walked on the rocky black earth.

T'Challa thought about the brass frogs. Who could create such things? If they were indeed teleportation devices, how did they work? Tafari had to have released the Originators using something. Whatever they were, he hoped he could use them to return home. Unfortunately, his planning had not gotten that far yet.

"I thought the Nether-Realms would be some kind of weird, interdimensional twilight zone," Zeke confessed.

"Uh," Shuri started, "would you rather deal with that?"

"No," Zeke said, looking around as he walked. "I'm glad this place just looks ordinary."

"We don't know what's ahead," T'Challa whispered. "Be on the lookout."

"Look," Sheila said, pointing into the distance.

A blanket of gray fog lay ahead of them.

T'Challa felt the weave of the Vibranium mesh in his suit tighten around his body. He sensed movement behind that veil of mist.

"What is it?" Zeke asked.

"Not sure," T'Challa said. "Walk slowly."

Shuri held her gauntlets up, ready for a threat.

T'Challa gripped the Scepter of Bast as he walked, his footfalls silent in the panther suit. As they advanced, the mist began to swirl around their feet.

"Guys?" Zeke said, looking at the ground, his voice high. "This doesn't seem too good."

The cool air gave way to a stuffy dampness. T'Challa was completely sealed by his suit, but still he felt it in the air, cloying and dense. Suddenly, the fog seemed to lift, as if it were a curtain being swept aside.

T'Challa's intake of breath could be heard clearly.

A gate stood ahead of them.

And past that gate, hundreds of Wakandans floated in midair, motionless, as if in some sort of suspended animation. Colossal bars rose up to an unseen roof.

"Bast protect us," Akema said.

Shuri scurried to the gate and shook the bars. "Father!" she shouted. "Mother!" She stepped back and thrust out both fists, ready to unleash a blast on the iron bars.

"No!" T'Challa cried out. "Wait. We may harm someone."

Shuri lowered her arms.

T'Challa stepped up and peered through the bars. It was as if the prisoners were asleep, floating in some kind of swirling substance. Blue and red lights flickered inside it. He tried to see faces, but they were all dark silhouettes, with no recognizable features. *Father is in there. Mother.*

"There has to be a way to get them out!" Sheila said.

T'Challa paused and tried to think. His father's voice echoed in his head.

Nothing is ever solved through anger.

I have to get them out, but how?

M'Baku suddenly scowled and tightened his grip on his spear. He stepped up and banged on one of the bars, creating a reverberation that sounded like a hundred bells ringing.

T'Challa gave him a side-eye. "M'Baku! *Wait.* No rash decisions!"

M'Baku stepped back. He knew T'Challa well, and that tone of voice was one he didn't hear often. "My parents are in there, too," M'Baku said, his face stoic.

"We'll get them out, M'Baku," T'Challa told him. "We will."

T'Challa wished he were as confident as his promise.

He studied the bars in front of him and the people trapped within them. *There has to be a way!* he shouted inside his head. He had to stay calm and focused, especially in front of everyone. If he suddenly accepted defeat, they would be lost. They were waiting for him—waiting for him to come up with an answer.

He reached out and touched one of the bars, which was cold and hot at the same time. An idea came to him, although he knew it might prove to be a deadly gambit.

"Shuri," he said, turning to face his sister.

"Yeah?"

"I want you to fire those gauntlets."

"Yes!" Shuri exclaimed. "Thought you'd never ask." She lifted her hands, ready to aim at the gate.

"At me," T'Challa said.

Shuri screwed up her face and turned back to her brother. "Yeah, right."

Sheila, Zeke, and M'Baku looked at their friend as if he had lost his mind.

"T'Challa," M'Baku said calmly. "What are you talking about?"

"My suit," T'Challa said. "It absorbs kinetic energy, right? That means I can store it up and then release it at a target."

Zeke raised an incredulous eyebrow. "So, let me get this straight. You want your sister to . . . *shoot* you with sonic energy so you can then break down this gate?"

"That's pretty much it," T'Challa replied.

"Great," Zeke said flatly. "Fantastic. The only Super Hero here, and he wants his sister to shoot him."

"It does make sense," Sheila put in. "If he absorbs enough energy, the impact should be pretty massive when it's released."

"I don't know about this, big bro," Shuri confessed. "I mean, not to brag, but I know this tech stuff pretty well, and the force might be enough to really mess you up."

"I've got to at least try it," T'Challa said.

"And what happens if you take *too* much damage?" Akema asked. "I am not sure of this, Prince. I do not think your father would approve."

"Well, he's not here," T'Challa said, and almost immediately regretted it.

There was a moment of silence.

"I'll be okay, Akema," T'Challa said. "I know it will work."

Akema relented and stepped back.

T'Challa faced Shuri and spread his arms wide, making a big target.

He put down the scepter and closed his eyes.

"You ready?" he asked.

CHAPTER
THIRTY-FOUR

Shuri aimed her gauntlets at T'Challa's chest. "If you die, I'll never forgive you."

T'Challa stood about five feet away from his sister, exposing his midsection, feet planted firmly apart. Sheila and Zeke looked on nervously. M'Baku stood silently, his face showing his distress. Akema looked away.

"You sure about this?" Shuri asked her brother once more.

"Nope," T'Challa said, and then: "On three."

Zeke closed his eyes.

"One . . ." T'Challa said, clenching his fists.

M'Baku backed up.

"Two . . ."

Shuri's hands were steady, but her face was anxious.

Here goes, T'Challa thought. "Three!"

The blast from Shuri's gauntlets sent T'Challa flying back several feet, dropping him to his knees.

"T'Challa!" Shuri cried out, rushing to his side. "Can you hear me?"

Akema was beside him in a flash.

"Of course I can hear you. I'm fine." He rose with a groan.

"What did it feel like?" Shuri asked.

"Like someone shot me with an energy blaster."

"Is that going to be enough?" Zeke asked. "Enough, er, energy?"

"I don't think so," T'Challa replied.

He stood up to his full height. Even though the blast had knocked him down, he didn't feel any ill effects. It was just weird to realize he had taken that much of a charge and was still conscious.

"Okay," he said, and twisted his neck from side to side. "Round two."

"That's enough!" Akema actually shouted. "The king and queen will have my head if I allow this to continue. This is madness!"

Her echo hung in the air like a threat.

Shuri released a tremulous sigh but also appeared ready to do whatever her brother wished. "I take responsibility, Akema. No harm will come to you. You have my word."

Akema shook her head, resigned to the fact that there was nothing she could do to stop these two royal kids.

"I'll be fine," T'Challa said. "Promise."

Sure am making a lot of promises, he thought.

Once again, T'Challa made himself big, arms outstretched, like a goalkeeper for a soccer team.

Shuri raised her hands. Sheila closed her eyes for a brief moment.

"Fire!" T'Challa shouted.

This blast seemed stronger than the first, and a wave of blue energy flowed from the gauntlets, knocking T'Challa on his backside.

"Another!" he cried out, raising his head, still on his knees.

"No!" Shuri shouted. "That's enough, T'Challa!"

But the young prince wasn't done yet.

"One more, Shuri, and that should be enough."

Shuri and the others traded worried glances.

"You sure?" Shuri asked him.

"Just do it!" T'Challa shouted.

Shuri raised her hands for what T'Challa could tell she hoped would be the third and final time.

"Fire!" T'Challa called.

Shuri gave one more blast.

This time, T'Challa toppled sideways and fell, completely, it seemed, unconscious.

"T'Challa!" Shuri cried.

"I knew this was a bad idea," Zeke said.

T'Challa lay with his eyes closed. He felt as if he had been hit by a bolt of lightning, which actually, was about right.

"Prince?" Akema said, kneeling down. She took his hand.

T'Challa opened his eyes. His head spun. "Help me up," he said with a grunt. "I don't want to lose the stored kinetic energy."

Akema and Shuri each grabbed a hand and pulled him to his feet. T'Challa felt the Vibranium mesh. A hole about the size of a small coin was burned into his suit.

"Not so bad," Shuri said, feeling the spot.

"Now," T'Challa said. "Let's see if this works."

He stood up and let out a long breath.

"Do you want to rest first?" Zeke asked.

"No time," T'Challa replied. "If we wait any longer, the energy will just dissipate."

T'Challa turned to face the gates. He felt the energy in his suit, waiting to be unleashed, pulsing and pulsing. . . .

He crossed his arms over his chest. "Wakanda forever!" he shouted, and then ran straight at the gate.

T'Challa didn't feel it at first, but a second later it hit him: A blast that split the gates asunder in a storm of smoke and debris. But he was still standing.

"My god," Sheila exclaimed.

The blast had sent the prisoners hurtling toward the

ground. Now they lay moaning and writhing, seemingly awake.

"Quickly!" T'Challa shouted. "See that they're all unharmed!"

At T'Challa's command, Akema and the others began checking on the freed Wakandans, helping them stand.

"Mother! T'Challa called, walking through the mass of confused people.

"Father!" Shuri cried out.

The now-free prisoners walked in circles, dazed and unsteady on their feet. Akema ran to some of her fellow Dora Milaje who had been swept up in the attack.

M'Baku froze where he stood.

A man was looking around, disoriented.

"Father," M'Baku said. "You're safe now."

He dropped his spear and hugged his father.

"M'Baku?" his father said, as if he didn't really know his own son.

"You're safe, Father. You're safe. Where's Mother?"

"Here I am," a weak voice called, as M'Baku's mother stumbled toward them.

"The festival," his father whispered, looking around. "There was a . . . an explosion. What happened?"

"Plenty of time to explain," his son said. "Let's get you out of here first."

T'Challa continued to call out, helped by his sister, while Zeke and Sheila tended to the others, giving calming words of support. T'Challa saw many familiar faces, elders of the community, his father's advisors, and the Dora Milaje, now weaponless. Everyone's clothing was torn and covered in dirt and black ooze.

A cry pierced the darkness.

T'Challa looked left, then right.

And then, like ghosts, several more people appeared out of the rubble.

Leading the way were an older man and woman, holding hands. T'Challa recognized them. They were the ones who were swept up when Tafari confronted T'Challa in Wakanda. The ones who looked as if they couldn't let go of each other.

Glory to Bast, they're all safe, T'Challa thought.

He gestured for help, and the rescued Wakandans found comfort among the others.

"T'Challa?"

T'Challa's ears twitched. He knew that voice.

"Mother?" he called. "Where are you?"

Shuri had heard the call as well, and rushed to her brother's side.

"There!" She pointed.

Several feet away, the queen stood alone, her once regal robes now marred with dirt.

T'Challa and his sister threw their arms around her. Sheila and Zeke looked on with smiling faces. It took several long moments for them to part.

"Father?" T'Challa said, breaking the embrace. "Where is he?"

A wave of worry passed over his mother's face.

"He was taken," she started. "Somewhere . . . somewhere else."

At that exact moment, the ground beneath T'Challa's feet began to tremble. He looked down. A few feet away, the black sand was swirling, like a dust devil picking up wind, building and building and building.

"Stand back!" T'Challa shouted, spreading his arms in front of his sister and mother.

The ground erupted in front of them with a great blast.

And then, creatures rose up from the depths.

CHAPTER
THIRTY-FIVE

They were hideous.

Human-shaped, but like some distant ancestor that time had forgotten, with horns on their heads and mouths crammed with deadly-looking teeth.

"Get them to safety!" T'Challa shouted, picking up his spear. "Quickly!"

"To me!" the queen cried out, leading the confused Wakandans away from the threat. "To me!"

The Dora Milaje, still fierce without their weapons, joined T'Challa and his companions, and he was glad for it. He needed all the help he could get.

T'Challa counted seven or eight of the strange beasts, but

it seemed like multitudes. There was no time for a plan—M'Baku, Shuri, and even Zeke and Sheila had no choice but to defend themselves as best they could.

T'Challa used the scepter as if he were born with it, raising it high and swinging down hard for an overhead attack, or spinning on his heel and using it low to the ground, tripping up his attackers. He took a lot of damage, but felt as if the suit still had kinetic energy stored up, making it even more of a barrier against attack.

M'Baku threw his mother her spear and she grasped it in midair, swinging it back into the midsection of one of the bizarre creatures. *Are they Originators as well,* T'Challa wondered, *or some other monstrosity from the depths?* Shuri blasted away with her gauntlets, sending blue shock waves at the incoming beasts.

Zeke and Sheila took cover in the chaos, darting here and there, throwing their detonators when they got a clear shot.

The beasts fought with wild swinging arms, but they were slow, and T'Challa calculated every one of their strikes with a dodge or counterattack. The real threat was their teeth, and so far, T'Challa and crew had evaded them.

But still, T'Challa was worried about Zeke and Sheila. M'Baku could hold his own, and Shuri had one of the most powerful weapons in Wakanda at her fingertips, but his friends only had the small discs.

T'Challa landed a roundhouse kick at one of the

creatures, and then jabbed the beast's midsection, sending it hurtling back. "Sheila! Zeke!" he called. "Follow my mother. Now!"

Zeke and Sheila, breathing hard, eyes terrified, didn't argue, and took off in the direction of the queen, but not before one last toss of their remaining missiles, which sent up clouds of smoke.

Now T'Challa had one less thing to worry about. He loved his friends and would never forgive himself if they were hurt . . . or worse. He was trained from the time he was a small child to be a fighter, as was his sister. There was no distinction in Wakanda between genders when it came to defending the nation.

The Dora Milaje fought as if battle were a symphony, a ballet of graceful moves and deadly crescendos.

Now T'Challa and his sister stood back-to-back, T'Challa pummeling the strange beings with kicks and leg sweeps, and maneuvering the scepter with both hands, while Shuri fired away with her gauntlets.

Finally, their enemy was defeated. Some fled, outnumbered, back into the darkness, while others lay motionless in the blasted black landscape.

M'Baku wiped his forehead with the back of his hand.

Shuri stood with her arms at her sides, exhausted from the tension of holding them up while continuously firing.

T'Challa sprinted toward his mother and the others, Shuri and M'Baku on his heels. His mother seemed to look at him anew. She glanced at her daughter, breathing hard. She opened her mouth to speak, but suddenly seemed to reconsider. There would be time for reprimands later, T'Challa imagined. Seeing his little sister with sonic gauntlets was probably something their mother had never imagined. Or would allow.

But still, T'Challa thought, *Shuri fought bravely, like a true warrior of Wakanda.*

T'Challa's breathing slowed, his heartbeat returning to normal.

"Prince," a woman's voice called.

It was Akema.

"We must rescue our king. We are sworn to protect him!"

"But where is he?" T'Challa pleaded.

"Look!" Zeke said, pointing behind T'Challa.

T'Challa spun around.

A figure was approaching in the darkness.

A ray of hope flared behind the queen's eyes.

T'Challa finally saw who it was, as T'Chaka, the King of Wakanda, collapsed in front of them.

CHAPTER
THIRTY-SIX

"Father," T'Challa said, kneeling down.

The king looked at his son, his eyes cloudy. "I was badly injured, T'Challa." He lifted his shirt, revealing his torso. A long gash leaked blood.

Ramonda gasped and knelt beside him. "We have to get him back to Wakanda! Now!"

T'Challa stood up while his mother and Shuri comforted his father.

"Sheila," T'Challa whispered. "Those frogs. Now's the time to see if they work. We have to get back."

Sheila reached into her bag and pulled out the gleaming objects, which seemed to light up the dark space by a fraction. King T'Chaka stirred. "King Solomon's Frogs? How did you come by . . . ?"

His head slumped back onto his chest.

"King Solomon?" Zeke whispered.

T'Challa had the same reaction, but there would be time for questions later. He handed the scepter to Zeke. "Hold on to this, Zeke. Don't lose it."

Zeke's mouth fell open as he grasped the mysterious spear.

Sheila handed T'Challa the two frogs. He hefted one in each hand. They had weight to them, heavier than one would imagine. "So," he said. "I guess I just—"

"Say the place you want to go," Zeke interrupted. "That's how it usually works in the comics and stuff."

T'Challa managed a weak smile. *What to say?* he wondered. *Aloud or to myself?*

He looked back to his father, whose head was being cradled by Ramonda. T'Challa saw his chest rise and fall as he took slow, deep breaths. *He has to be okay. He has to be.*

T'Challa raised the objects above his head, one in each hand. "To whoever holds the power of these . . . King Solomon's Frogs, take us back to our home. Wakanda. Take us from this place."

He tapped the two frogs together and hesitantly lowered his arms. A slight tingle raced along his palms and up his wrists. The frogs began to vibrate in his hands, a tremor that ran through his whole body. He felt as if the black rock under his feet was moving.

T'Challa heard a whooshing sound in his ears, and felt wind on his face. A blur of images raced across his vision, all too fast to comprehend. He felt himself hurtling through a tunnel of sorts. He wasn't aware of anyone else with him, but he sensed a presence all around him at the same time, as if he wasn't alone on this journey.

The blackness was overwhelming. And cold. He wanted to wrap his arms around himself, but he felt disconnected, out of his own body. He remembered that once, when he was a small child, his father had taken him to an isolation tank. That was where the Black Panther relaxed and focused after a difficult battle or decision. After adding several hundred pounds of salt to water, the human body floats, setting the mind free in the darkness. Young T'Challa didn't hesitate to get in, as he wished for nothing more than to be like his father. He remembered settling into the warm water and floating into a watery bliss. This was the same feeling he had now, as he spun through time and space.

He opened his eyes.

They were back in Wakanda. T'Challa balanced himself. His head was dizzy. He clutched something in both hands. He looked down. The frogs cycled through a myriad of colors and then went back to brass, the gemstone eyes blinking red.

T'Challa watched as more and more Wakandans came through, all accompanied by a flash of blinding white light.

"We did it!" Shuri cried. "It worked!"

Zeke, Sheila, and M'Baku tumbled through all at once, a tangle of arms and legs. Fortunately, Zeke still held the scepter.

"Oof!" Sheila moaned. "Get off of me, Zeke!"

"Sorry," Zeke said, unknotting his arm from the crook of Sheila's leg. "It's not every day you get sent through some crazy portal." He stood up and rubbed his jaw. "Feels like I left my teeth back there." He handed T'Challa the scepter.

T'Challa looked for his father and mother. They had already come through, as had several others, including the Dora Milaje.

"T'Challa," his mother said breathlessly. "What did you do? How did we . . . ?" She trailed off.

"I'll have to explain later, Mother. Do not worry."

The queen looked around, amazed, as if she had never seen Wakanda before.

"Dora Milaje!" Akema cried out, a rallying cry to her sisters. Immediately, the ragtag group snapped to attention. "Lead the king and queen to the palace. Nareema and Ayanda will stay behind with me."

"Good idea," T'Challa said. "We don't want any of those creatures coming through behind us."

"What do we do now?" Zeke asked.

T'Challa clutched the scepter. "We have to find Tafari. And then I'm going to send those Originators back to the Nether-Realms."

CHAPTER
THIRTY-SEVEN

"T'Challa," his father said as he was helped up by the queen, "do not use those brass frogs again. They are dangerous."

T'Challa drew close to him.

"They distort time and space, son. We're lucky we're all still alive."

Sheila looked at T'Challa, shocked.

"Where do they come from?" T'Challa asked. "I have so much to tell you. I . . ."

The king's shoulders sagged, and Ramonda and Nareema held him up.

T'Challa inhaled a short breath. He had never seen his father in such a bad state before.

Ramonda turned to T'Challa. She laid a comforting hand on his cheek. "I will not tell you what to do, my son. But be careful. The nation needs you."

T'Challa held his mother's hand for a moment before they departed. Shuri, accompanied by a few of the Dora Milaje, led the way. T'Challa watched them leave, feeling his father's pain as they did so.

M'Baku's mother handed her spear back to her son. "You threw it to me in the nick of time, M'Baku. It has served me well. Now it is your time to wield it. You've proved your worth."

M'Baku took the spear gently, as if it might break. "Thank you, Mother. I will bear it with honor."

T'Challa watched them walk away until they were out of sight. He took a deep breath, readying himself for the next phase of the rescue.

"Where are the two trees?" Sheila suddenly exclaimed. "Those frogs didn't send us to the right place!"

T'Challa and the others looked around. Sheila was right, he realized. The last few moments were so startling and confusing he hadn't even noticed where, exactly, they were.

"So they *are* tricky," T'Challa whispered.

"What's tricky?" asked Zeke.

"Those brass frogs," T'Challa replied. "Father said they distort time and space, and that we're lucky to be alive."

Zeke gulped. "Jeez. They could have teleported us to the middle of the Amazon or something!"

T'Challa didn't understand the frogs, and now wasn't the time to try to figure them out. "Hold on to these," T'Challa said, handing Sheila the frogs.

She took them carefully, as if they were about to send them through another dimension, and placed them in her bag.

"How are we going to do this?" Sheila asked. "If we can't use these frogs, how are we going to send those Originators back to where they came from?"

T'Challa grinned. "Good thing we have another way." He caressed the claw around his neck. "If it sent us to the Nether-Realms, it can surely send someone back, right?"

"Right," Zeke said.

"Then that's what we'll do," T'Challa finished. "Once we find Tafari, I'll use the Claw of Bast and send those monsters back from where they came."

"But first we have to find the trees," Sheila said.

Akema shaded her eyes with her hand. "West," she said. "A few miles."

T'Challa looked at her, amazed.

"I know my country like the back of my hand, Prince," she said.

"Good," T'Challa said. "Let's go."

Akema sent Nareema and Ayanda to the rear while she took up the lead.

They were on the edges of a forest, that much T'Challa knew. But the landscape didn't look familiar to him. He had to trust in Akema. She said she knew the way.

T'Challa felt vulnerable out in the open, with nothing but trees to hide their approach. Tafari was surely planning his next move. All T'Challa had to do was beat him to it.

Time seemed to slow as they walked. T'Challa wondered how many hours had passed between when they entered the Nether-Realms through the portal and their return. The sun was still in the same position as when they had left. He looked back at his friends. Their steps were slowing, and their faces showed their exhaustion.

"Let's rest a moment," T'Challa said after a half hour.

He called to Akema, and she gathered her sisters together to keep an eye out. There was no rest for the Dora Milaje. T'Challa really wasn't sure what to say to Nareema and Ayanda. He wanted to ask them about their experience in the Nether-Realms but decided against it. The memory was probably still too close. Who knew what horrors they faced? They hardly ever spoke at the palace, and he didn't think now was the time for small talk.

Zeke and Sheila needed no further encouragement to stop, and immediately came to a halt and rested, their backs up against tall trees. M'Baku sat down with a heavy sigh. The shade cooled their faces.

T'Challa sat, but remained tense and on edge. His friends were wiped out. "You guys did a good job back there," he said. "I know it was scary. I'm proud of all of you."

"Yeah," M'Baku put in. "Nice job with those little bombs."

Zeke managed a smile.

"We stick together," Sheila said. "We always have."

Sheila's comment brought a smile to T'Challa's face. He reflected on his first meeting with Zeke and Sheila. His father had sent him and M'Baku to Chicago after discovering Wakanda was under a possible attack. Zeke had been one of the first people to speak to him, and they became fast friends soon after. T'Challa had met him on the local bus, his nose buried in a graphic novel. A short time later, he met Sheila. Her smarts and quick wit were immediately evident, and her battles with Zeke on the most ridiculous of subjects soon endeared them both to him.

As the sun descended a little lower, they continued their trek. A cool breeze came and quickly dissipated. Even in the midst of their dire situation, T'Challa almost nodded off. He shook his head, coming to his senses. *One day I will rest. Soon, I hope.*

The journey was taking much longer than T'Challa would have thought, but he had to keep moving forward. It was definitely more than the few miles Akema had described.

The ground became more rocky and uneven, and the sky was quickly darkening. The Dora Milaje marched effortlessly, and even T'Challa had to speed up his stride to stay in time with them. His throat was parched. He gazed back at Zeke and Sheila. It looked to T'Challa as if they were barely hanging on. *They're doing this for me*, he realized. *They could have gone back to the safety of home but instead decided to stay and help. I couldn't ask for better friends.*

T'Challa continued to march. He reflected on all he and his friends had already done. They had rescued his parents and made sure they were safe, along with the other Wakandans who had been captured. But now wasn't the time for a pat on the back. Not until Tafari and the Originators were defeated.

After a while, T'Challa saw the familiar white cliffs of the Valley of the Kings.

Zeke let out a sigh of relief.

"We approach," Akema said.

T'Challa was relieved. He could see the moringa trees not too far up ahead. He clutched the claw around his neck.

A flock of birds exploded from a stand of trees, and T'Challa and the others flinched. An eerie silence descended. The sensors in T'Challa's suit pulsed. Akema held up a closed fist in warning.

"What is it?" Zeke whispered.

T'Challa scanned the area. "Not sure. I thought I sensed movement."

Akema looked at T'Challa, and her green eyes were startled.

"We've been seen," she whispered.

CHAPTER
THIRTY-EIGHT

With a bloodcurdling cry, a dozen or more Simbi and Anansi rushed from the forest.

T'Challa's legs felt as if they were going to go out from under him. They were outnumbered. There was no way they could defeat this many, even with Akema and her fighters.

"Looks like they brought the fight to us, T'Challa," M'Baku said. He gripped his spear and readied himself. Zeke and Sheila stood motionless, looking to T'Challa for a command.

But someone beat T'Challa to it.

"For the king!" Akema cried out as she and her sisters dashed forward.

T'Challa hefted the Scepter of Bast. "For Wakanda!" he called, and joined the fray.

Zeke and Sheila, unarmed and shaking with fear, fled for the safety of the surrounding trees.

With the Scepter of Bast, your enemies will flee before you.

"Back!" T'Challa shouted, and drove the scepter into the earth.

The blast sent the creatures flying in a great gust of wind. T'Challa couldn't stop and wonder at the power of the scepter; instead, he took advantage of their retreat, while the Dora Milaje continued their assault.

But right at that moment, a surge of more of the hideous beasts came through the forest, like ants climbing up from their colony. There were dozens of them, armed with spears. The Anansi, the dreadful spiders, shot webs from their mouths. M'Baku, fighting as fiercely as he could, became entangled.

"Help!" he cried. "T'Challa!"

But T'Challa had his own problem. He was being overcome by the Simbi.

They circled him, jabbing and thrusting their spears, which T'Challa imagined to be tipped with deadly venom.

"For Wakanda!" a small voice shouted, and Zeke ran out from his hiding place. He tried to untangle the webs around M'Baku, clawing at him with his small hands.

"Get back, Zeke!" M'Baku shouted as one of the Anansi knocked the diminutive figure of Zeke aside.

Zeke scuttled back on his heels and elbows.

T'Challa broke free of the Simbi, but he was dizzy and fatigued. Had he been stabbed? His mind raced with fear and adrenaline.

We're not going to make it. The thought suddenly dawned on him. *It's too late.*

But all was not lost.

M'Baku fought his way free of the deadly spider creatures and rushed to T'Challa's side.

"We have to do something now!" M'Baku shouted. "We can't hold them much longer!"

Time seemed to slow down for T'Challa at that moment. The battle was a blur in front of him. He saw each and every one of the dreadful creatures' faces snarling and hissing. Would they be the last faces he would ever see?

Akema and her sisters fought with bravery, but they, too, were being overwhelmed.

A rumbling above them drew T'Challa's attention. *What new threat is this?* he thought.

But as T'Challa looked up, hope flared in his heart.

The afterburners of the king's personal aircraft, the Royal Talon Fighter, flashed red. A tornado of debris lifted from the ground as the ship landed in a cloud of shimmering heat.

And as T'Challa watched, with the battle raging around him, the Black Panther, dressed in his ceremonial mantle, leapt from the ship, a battalion of Dora Milaje at his command.

"Yibambe!" a chorus of voices called.

"Yibambe!"

"It's the Wakandan battle cry!" Zeke shouted.

And as the Originators turned to face this new threat, T'Challa smiled.

The Dora Milaje, armed with Vibranium spears, fell upon the invaders with deadly force, driving them back. Shuri was with them, and had exchanged her gauntlets for Ring Blades, Vibranium-made hoops that could be used in close combat or thrown to stun an attacker. Best of all, like a boomerang, they returned to the owner after hitting their mark.

"Yes!" Zeke and Sheila cried out, still taking shelter.

T'Challa caught his father's glance as they fought side by side, father and son, king and prince, together.

T'Challa struck out with the scepter, using every move he could muster to rid the nation of the vile creatures.

The Dora Milaje were at the forefront, and they whirled, kicked, and dove upon the enemy, giving the Originators no chance to evade their acrobatic maneuvers.

M'Baku shouted as he fought, his spear twirling.

The words of the Three rang in T'Challa's head:

Seal them in the Nether-Realms and lock the gate. The time will come only once. Sheila must have had the same thought as T'Challa, and she cried out from where she and Zeke had taken cover. "Over here, T'Challa! By the trees!"

T'Challa turned at the sound of her voice, and then

dodged a blow by one of the Simbi. "Father!" he shouted. "Drive them this way!"

King T'Chaka gave his son a quizzical look, but trusted T'Challa's command. "This way!" King T'Chaka bellowed. "To me!"

Every Wakandan fighter followed his command.

T'Challa ran toward Sheila and Zeke, standing near the trees, the enemy only steps behind him.

It must have looked like a retreat to the Originators, until M'Baku, Akema, and several Dora Milaje turned around, creating a defensive line in front of T'Challa and the advancing horde.

"Hold the line!" Akema shouted. "My king, drive them this way!"

The Black Panther heard Akema's call and drove the beasts forward.

With Akema and his father at his back, T'Challa turned around, facing the space between the trees. The clash of battle sounded behind him. He had to be quick. He snatched the chain from his neck. "I call on Kokou, the Ever-Burning, God of War! I call on Thoth, God-Bird; Ibis the Invincible; the Lord of Divine Words. And I call on Bast the almighty, She of Sun and Moon, the Devouring One. . . . Send these creatures back to the depths!"

T'Challa ran the claw down the invisible door.

Instantly, a gaping hole of blinding light opened in the darkening forest, blue and red light winking within. He dove to the side, clattering into Zeke and Sheila as the Simbi and Anansi were pulled through in a powerful vacuum, serpentine tails slithering and pincers clawing at empty air.

King T'Chaka and his fighters followed T'Challa's lead and parted left and right, leaving the creatures off guard to be drawn through the portal.

"Now!" Shuri shouted. "Seal the gate!"

T'Challa leapt back up, steering clear of the terrible pull of the portal. *How to seal the gate? No one ever told me how.*

"Use the claw!" Zeke shouted.

Zeke was right, T'Challa realized. He had used it before to open the doorway. Couldn't it also be used to close it?

The light was blinding, accompanied by a ringing that seemed to split his ears.

"Join hands!" the Black Panther called out.

T'Challa was confused. What was his father doing? But it only took him a moment to understand.

A human chain of sorts was being formed away from the opening of the gate with Zeke, Sheila, M'Baku, and Akema and her fighters. The last in the line was King T'Chaka. The force of the portal was tremendous and they dug their heels in to keep from being pulled forward. "Take my hand, T'Challa!" his father shouted.

T'Challa grasped his father's hand. He was in front of the door now, but the tug-of-war line behind him prevented him from being drawn in.

He could see the Simbi and Anansi on the other side, but

their forms seemed insubstantial, like ghosts. They writhed and hissed at each other in a kind of panicked frenzy.

T'Challa had to hurry.

While his father and all those in line held back his weight, preventing him from sliding through, T'Challa drew an X with the claw, much like the Wakandan greeting over the door. Leaves and debris flew up in a whirlwind.

A bright light, so brilliant it lit up the whole forest, exploded from the portal, sending T'Challa and the others reeling back.

And then it was done.

The gate was sealed.

The silence that followed was palpable.

T'Challa, along with everyone else, picked himself up. Zeke pumped his fist in the air. "Yes!" he shouted, and then looked embarrassed. A stillness permeated the forest. Even the leaves on the trees seemed to freeze, as if stuck in a moment in time. The bodies of the Originators who hadn't been sucked through the gate lay crumpled and motionless. T'Challa had to turn away from the gruesome display.

A cry sounded to T'Challa's left.

He spun around quickly.

Ayanda and Nareema appeared from the other side of the forest. But they were not alone.

Tafari and Professor Silumko, hands bound, were pushed to the ground just a few feet away from T'Challa and his father.

"There are more of them," Nareema said. "With your leave, my king, we will track them."

The Black Panther nodded once, and Ayanda and Nareema fled back into the woods.

Tafari looked up with wide eyes, stricken by fear. His once-white robes were filthy. Sweat and blood marred his brow. Silumko hung his head in defeat, not meeting T'Challa's or the king's eyes.

"My king!" Tafari exclaimed in a frantic voice, looking to the Black Panther. "They forced me! The invaders. They said they would give me power!"

T'Challa didn't believe him for a moment, but still, whether it was an act or not, tears were on Tafari's cheeks.

"Forgive me, King T'Chaka. I am a loyal Wakandan. I never—"

"Silence, Tafari!" T'Challa hissed. "You don't have the right to speak to the king."

The Black Panther froze where he stood. He was staring at Tafari with an intensity T'Challa had never seen before.

"Father?" T'Challa said. "What is it?"

The Black Panther continued to stare, never once taking his eyes off Tafari groveling in the dirt. "This boy," he said in a faraway voice. "I know who he is."

CHAPTER
THIRTY-NINE

"It was long ago," King T'Chaka said to T'Challa.

T'Challa and his father sat in the throne room. The king appeared weary, his face drawn. Tafari and Silumko had already been interrogated by the king and now both sat detained in a locked room guarded by the Dora Milaje. Tafari's disciples were also being detained.

"I don't understand," T'Challa said. "You know him? Who is he?"

King T'Chaka rubbed his brow. "When you were a child, only a year old or so, Tafari's father challenged me for the throne. His name was Hodari."

T'Challa cocked his head. "Hodari? I've never heard the name."

King T'Chaka sighed. "Many have challenged me for the throne, son, but I have remained victorious all these years, glory to Bast."

T'Challa nodded. "So, what happened? With this man, Hodari?"

King T'Chaka's jawline flexed, a nervous habit T'Challa had noticed several times before. "Hodari was a great warrior, a leader of the Jabari. We dueled for the throne in ceremonial combat."

T'Challa had heard tales of his father's victories, but this one was new to him.

"He was strong," King T'Chaka continued, "and I thought I might fall. But, at the last moment, I pinned him. He couldn't move, T'Challa. But he would . . . not . . . yield."

King T'Chaka looked *through* T'Challa, as if he were not there in the room with him but locked in combat all those years ago.

"'Yield!' I demanded," King T'Chaka hissed through gritted teeth. "'*Yield*, Hodari!' But my cry went unheeded. Instead, Hodari reached into his tunic. A blade was hidden there—a blade from the White Gorilla Cult."

T'Challa had a sudden memory—the knife he'd seen in his father's wardrobe, with the bared fangs of a gorilla, the Jabari tribe's sigil.

"Instead of accepting defeat, he drew the blade across his throat."

T'Challa gasped.

"I released my grip on him, and the knife fell from his hand. His family never forgave me, T'Challa, thinking it was I who had delivered the killing blow."

T'Challa hung his head a moment, giving his father time to recover. It seemed as if just telling the tale had fatigued him even further. "But ceremonial combat for the throne always ends in death for the defeated. Doesn't it?"

King T'Chaka's jawline flexed again. "Not always, T'Challa. I would not have killed Hodari if he had not yielded. Sometimes the old ways need to be changed." There was silence for a moment. King T'Chaka exhaled a labored breath.

"How did you know it was him?" T'Challa asked after a moment. "Tafari. How did you know he was Hodari's son?"

King T'Chaka nodded. "I knew his family. He was a proud man and had just celebrated the birth of his first son. He named him Tafari. The same name you used when you shouted for him to be silent."

T'Challa shook his head. It all made sense now. Tafari resented the Royal Family and Wakanda for the death of his father. His family must have spread the mistruth, and Tafari was the one to suffer for it. He wanted a new Wakanda,

T'Challa recalled, one free from the Panther Cult and all its trappings.

It is time for a new generation, Tafari had said . . . *one untethered from the curse of Vibranium and all the turmoil it has brought.*

"He told me that this . . . Professor Silumko egged him and the other students on," King T'Chaka continued, "told them that Wakanda had a secret history, one that they could claim, if they only rose up."

T'Challa thought back to his meeting with the professor and his evasive manner. "What will happen to them?" he asked.

"I can't condemn Tafari now," King T'Chaka said. "To do so would be a cruelty I cannot abide."

T'Challa stood up. "But . . . but you could have died, Father! You and Mother, and all the others. He brought those monsters here!"

King T'Chaka's face was solemn in the darkness of the throne room. "I will find a solution. They have both wrought great havoc, and it cannot go unpunished."

Reluctantly, T'Challa knew his father was right. Being a king meant acting wisely and justly, not out of anger and revenge.

"The same goes for the others," the king continued. "They are young, T'Challa. I have to think on this. What would cause such rebellion under my rule?"

The king rested his forehead on a closed fist.

T'Challa could feel his pain. This revolt had occurred under his father's reign. *How will I rule? What would I do in this situation?*

T'Challa told his father all about the failed revolt and how it had played out in Wakanda: his surreal encounters in the Necropolis, finding Zawavari, and seeing King Azzuri the Wise. The king listened quietly, nodding now and then, totally engaged by his son's revelations.

"The Three," T'Challa said. "They didn't say who they were, other than calling themselves the Guardians of the Temple and the Keepers of the Claw of Bast. Do you know?"

King T'Chaka studied him for a moment. "I can only guess, son. I may be king, but there are mysteries in Wakanda even I do not have the answer to. I would imagine they are Wakandan priests of old who have somehow withstood the ravages of time, here to help us in our time of need."

"What about those frogs?" T'Challa continued. He had so many questions he couldn't get them out fast enough. "You said something about King Solomon. What are they?"

The Black Panther leaned back. "Ah, yes. King Solomon's Frogs. They are exactly what you suspect they are—mysterious devices that bend time and space. They are ancient totems, thousands of years old. You were very lucky, T'Challa. I have heard stories that these objects have a mind of their own, and don't always follow their owner's demands. They have a long and interesting history."

T'Challa eased out a breath, glad that the frogs hadn't sent him and his friends to the ends of the earth. "Where did Tafari get them? The frogs."

The king grinned. "He said that the professor knew their whereabouts, sealed in a Vibranium vault. He had been searching for many years and unearthed them in the ruins of a temple. I now have them in a safe place, too," T'Challa said, "that should be put away as well. Things from the . . . the Orishas. I will bring them here for safekeeping."

"You are fortunate to have them gifted to you," the king said. "Surely it is a sign that you are blessed by the gods."

T'Challa swallowed, and felt a stinging behind his eyes. What he had seen and experienced in the Temple of Bast was extraordinary, and yet his father believed him, and even . . .

"The . . . Originators," T'Challa started. "Did you know of them? I had never heard of them in my studies."

"I had heard tales from the elders," T'Chaka replied, "but never imagined it could truly be real. I was wrong."

T'Challa had one more question, and he asked it tentatively. "Father. The Nether-Realms. What happened there?"

"There are things in the unseen world, T'Challa. Things better left undisturbed. The Nether-Realms lead to deeper, darker worlds. I had to use all of my strength and wit to escape, or be trapped there for eternity." A shadow seemed

---

"It is, Father. They said it was the Claw of Bast. I will give it to you for safekeeping." He reached for the chain to remove it from his neck.

"Don't," his father said. "I think it suits you." He paused. "Young Panther."

T'Challa's heart swelled as he turned back around.

As he left the throne room, he passed Akema, standing guard. She glanced his way and gave a brief nod. But it felt different this time. It seemed to be a gesture of respect.

pass over his face. T'Challa knew right then his father would never speak of it again.

"I am glad you are home, Father. You and Mother."

"Glory to Bast," his father replied, "that our Vibranium technology healed me quickly, and that I was able to return to help you. Although, if I may say, I think you were faring quite well even before my arrival."

T'Challa didn't comment, but offered a weak smile.

"We wouldn't be here without you, son. *And your sister and your friends.* You did what a true leader must, and for that, I am proud."

"I could have done more," T'Challa admitted. "Tafari made a threat before the festival. I brushed it aside and then . . ."

King T'Chaka interrupted him. "But you learned a valuable lesson as well, didn't you?"

"What?" T'Challa asked. "What lesson?"

The king leaned forward, his brown eyes fierce. "Never underestimate a threat."

"Yes, sir," T'Challa said. "I never will again."

T'Challa gave a slight bow of his head and turned to leave.

"T'Challa," his father called to his re

T'Challa turned around.

"That claw arou

Orishas as

CHAPTER FORTY

T'Challa, Sheila, and Zeke lounged in T'Challa's private quarters. Platters of grilled meats, vegetables, and bread were laid out before them, as well as a few ice-cold pitchers of Kola Kola.

"This is more like it," Zeke said, stuffing his mouth with another sweet fig. "I expected lots of tasty treats and new cuisine on this trip, but all I got was a bunch of snake men."

T'Challa winced. Even though the threat was over, images of the dreadful Simbi and Anansi were still present in his mind.

The Wakandan network was back up, thanks to the techs at the science lab. It seemed that Tafari and Professor

Silumko had used Vibranium-enhanced malware along with an electromagnetic pulse to knock it out.

"So, we've only got a few more days to hang out," Sheila said. "What should we do?"

T'Challa wasn't sure if he was up for anything. He wanted to have fun with his friends these few remaining days, but he couldn't put it all behind him just yet. Their trip to Wakanda would be one they'd never forget, for good or ill.

"I just need to rest a while longer, guys," T'Challa said. "I'm sorry."

His friends gave him sympathetic smiles. Could they sense how emotionally drained he was, inside and out?

When they finally left, T'Challa slept, and he dreamt of gods and monsters.

Zeke sped alongside T'Challa, his hover bike at full throttle. "Can't catch me!" he screamed into the wind as he zipped past.

Sheila, a comfortable distance behind both, shook her head. "Boys," she whispered.

T'Challa raced to catch up. He was glad his friends were having some fun on their last few days. Sheila even got a visit to the science labs, with Shuri as a chaperone. The king had made a special invitation after her "service to the nation."

As for T'Challa, he was feeling pretty good, and the ordeal of the past few days was no longer at the forefront of his mind.

He could have easily passed Zeke, but T'Challa hung back just to give Zeke the thrill of winning. They all came to a stop near Lake Turkana, the same as they had done before all the madness started.

"That was fun!" Zeke exclaimed.

"Should have stayed with Shuri in the lab," Sheila complained.

T'Challa wiped beads of sweat from his forehead. The sun was high and brilliant, and the cool breezes coming off the lake were a relief.

They all left their bikes and walked down to the water's edge. Zeke took off his shoes and walked in the golden sand.

"There's something I need to tell you guys," T'Challa said.

Zeke and Sheila froze, ready for some terrible news.

"Oh. Sorry," T'Challa apologized. "It's nothing bad. My father is having a celebration tonight, and you two are invited!"

Zeke's eyes went wide. "What kind of food will be there?"

"Really?" Sheila put in, giving Zeke a side-eye.

"Anything you want, Zeke," T'Challa said. "But I doubt there'll be Southern MoonPies."

"Maybe I can teach someone how to make one," Zeke said. "That cool chef. What was her name? Gloria?"

T'Challa shook his head, laughing. "Yeah, it's Gloria. If

you know all the ingredients I can tell her. I'm sure she'll put her own spin on it, too."

Zeke licked his lips.

Later that night, T'Challa met up with Zeke and Sheila, and they headed to an area not far from the palace. They gathered in an open space near a hillside with windswept trees and flowering plants. People were everywhere, singing and dancing, offering free food, which Zeke immediately took an interest in. It was a peaceful antidote to the troubles that had befallen the country.

M'Baku and Shuri joined them near a special place reserved for the king and queen. And as the sun began to set, red and orange blazed across the sky. Musicians took up the drums, and the pulse of Wakanda floated out over the crowd.

"Ain't no party like a Wakanda party," Zeke said, snagging a morsel from a man passing by with a tray of treats.

"What is it?" Sheila asked, wondering what Zeke had just eaten.

"No idea," Zeke replied, popping it into his mouth.

King T'Chaka and Queen Ramonda walked among the crowd, greeting each person they passed with a warm smile. The Dora Milaje, ever vigilant, kept a careful eye on their surroundings all the same.

"So," King T'Chaka said, stopping in front of T'Challa and his friends. "I guess we have you two to thank as well."

Zeke almost choked on his food. "Uh, yes, sir," he started. "I mean . . . uh . . ."

"It was an honor to be here," Sheila said, coming to the rescue. "T'Challa's our best friend, and he's helped us out in ways we can't even count."

"Good," Queen Ramonda said. "We're glad he has friends he can really trust. You mean a lot to him."

T'Challa fidgeted a little, embarrassed. Shuri laughed.

"We want to give you something as a memento of your trip to Wakanda," King T'Chaka said.

Sheila and Zeke both went still, trying to hide their excitement.

Queen Ramonda looked at one of the Dora Milaje, who brought her a small box.

"This is a thank-you from the nation," King T'Chaka said.

"Thank you," Zeke and Sheila said at the same time. Sheila took the box in her hands. It was small and black and covered in crushed velvet.

"Well, open it!" Shuri exclaimed.

Sheila handed it to Zeke. "You do it," she said.

Zeke took the box and, being as respectful as possible in the king and queen's presence, opened it slowly and tried to stifle his excitement.

"Wow!" he whisper-shouted.

Sheila leaned in.

Inside the box, two rings were revealed. Zeke drew one out and handed the other to Sheila.

"These rings have a stone made from Vibranium," the Black Panther said. "Not enough for technological use, but still, consider yourselves the only Americans to have a bit of Wakanda's most valuable metal."

"Aside from Captain America," T'Challa reminded them. Sheila had to nudge Zeke to close his mouth.

Zeke slipped the ring on his finger and held it up. A small gray stone seemed to wink a little in the failing light.

"It's beautiful," Sheila said, turning her wrist like a hand model.

"The nation thanks you," Queen Ramonda said.

T'Challa smiled at his parents' generosity.

"We have more guests to greet," the king said, and to T'Challa's surprise, brought his arms up to his chest. "Wakanda forever, Zeke."

Zeke froze. He swallowed. His face seemed to go through a multitude of expressions all in one instance. Finally, he returned the gesture. "Wakanda forever . . . sir."

The Black Panther chuckled and led the queen away.

"Well," Sheila said, "this is . . . I don't think I'll ever forget this moment."

"Not ever," Zeke said, hypnotized by the glinting ring on his finger. "Not . . . ever."

That night, while his friends slept, T'Challa walked to his favorite place—the Oasis. The cool breeze and the gently swaying reeds seemed a balm to his soul. He thought about everything he had been through. He had seen the Orishas, for Bast's sake. Was it a dream?

It did *happen,* he told himself. The Claw, Scepter, and Eye of Bast were proof. "The Eye," he whispered. He had used the claw and the scepter, but never the ring.

He took the Eye of Bast from his pocket.

With the Eye of Bast, you will see into the beyond.

He held it up to the night sky. The full moon filled the circle with a glow. And within that glow he saw a vision. A vision where he sat on the Panther Throne as the protector of Wakanda. He felt, just for a moment, the power of the Panther Goddess, Bast, pulsing through his veins.

He wanted to run through the Valley of the Kings and feel the earth under his thundering feet. He wanted to open his mouth and roar.

He was King T'Challa, son of T'Chaka, grandson of King Azzuri the Wise.

He was the Black Panther.

Long live the king.

The End